RESCUE

PARADISE TO INFERNO

SHREEJIT NAIR

notionpress.com

INDIA • SINGAPORE • MALAYSIA

Notion Press

Old No. 38, New No. 6
McNichols Road, Chetpet
Chennai - 600 031

First Published by Notion Press 2015
Reprint by Notion Press 2020
Copyright © Shreejit Nair 2020
All Rights Reserved.

ISBN 978-9-38487-873-3

Acknowledgements

Life has often kept me occupied with stories that fine-tune my imagination. The world of fiction has always belittled my problems and failures. As a writer, whenever I create a new world with the power of my mind, I feel blessed. As we all say, he who is the creator of all resides within each one of us. Thank you, God, for bestowing your divine blessings and helping me in coming up with good ideas and thoughts. Though my becoming an author was never on the cards, it has happened, and I am extremely happy about it. The story of *Rescue*, the minute it came into my mind, was a momentous experience; I decided to pen it down so that it remains with me for all time. I would like to thank a few special people who helped me to overcome every obstacle I came across my path.

I would like to thank my parents for always encouraging my creative work. Though the book came as a surprise to them, I don't have words to describe their reaction when they came to know that their son was an author. Mummy and Papa...I love you.

I sincerely thank my teacher, Mrs. Sunita Ghosh, who helped in encouraging the poet inside me. Ma'am, I am sure you will be happy to know that I am an author now. I thank my teacher, Mr. Prateek Jain, a brilliant author himself who guided me towards the right path on how to publish my book. Thank you, sir, for supporting a beginner like me especially when I struggled for almost a year to publish it.

A big, loving thanks and a great hug to my dearest friend Ghananshu Dwivedi (Anshul), without whom the book would have been still a dream. I started writing this book long back and took four years to complete it. I may have added a few more years if not for his help. Thank you, Anshul, for helping me with the plot of the story and also advising me to get under the skin of a 17-year-old to write this story and make it more believable. Thank you brother... you rock!

I would like to express my sincere gratitude to Notion Press for their efficient publishing program, to my editor, Ms. Poornima Narayanan, for her constant efforts in making the book look good and error free, and to my publishing manager, Ms. Dhanya Kaydar, for her skilful management of things and standing as a strong bridge between me and everything.

Last but not the least... thank you to those helping hands that unknowingly guided me somewhere, sometime along the way.

*Those who make peaceful revolution impossible
make violent revolution inevitable.*

– JOHN. F. KENNEDY

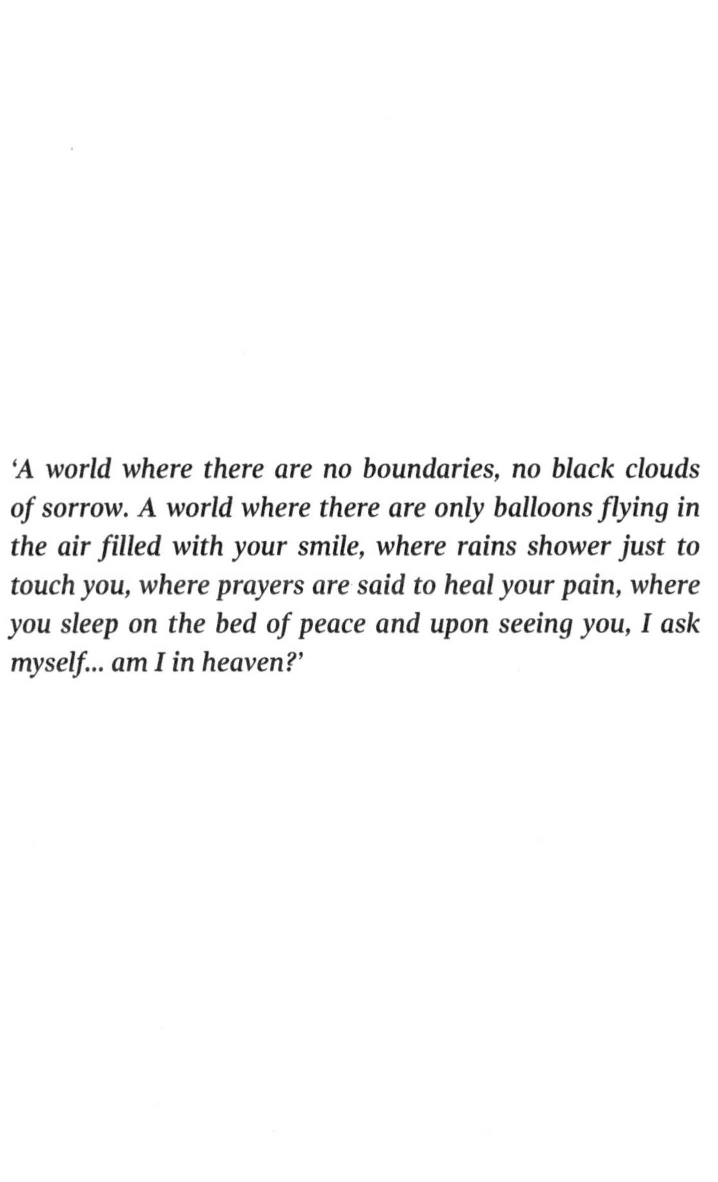

'A world where there are no boundaries, no black clouds of sorrow. A world where there are only balloons flying in the air filled with your smile, where rains shower just to touch you, where prayers are said to heal your pain, where you sleep on the bed of peace and upon seeing you, I ask myself... am I in heaven?'

Prologue

The wheels of the Capital Express rolled on the dead, flat railway tracks simultaneously with the spinning of the time wheel. It was 6:30 am and the passengers were loath to wake up on a cold and chilly morning in December. Winter in New Delhi starts from the end of November and continues till March. The cold waves sweeping down from the Himalayan region make for biting cold weather. Temperatures drop substantially, to as low as 3º C to 4º C during peak winter. The nights get really frosty and bonfires are lit all around the streets to bear with the cold. Usually though, daytime in winter is pleasant, with bright sunlight in the afternoons.

The loud and the roaring sound of the train horn disturbed the sleep of the cold-drenched environment. Tearing apart the cold winds with its bullet-like speed and carrying a heavy weight of people, projecting its great mechanical efficiency, the train was about to reach its destination. Some passengers were still inside their sheets, shivering and trembling, some overpowered by the forces of cold and sleep while others were already up at their regular waking time. They had already started taking their morning refreshments, as if imposed with some kind of strict army discipline.

A man sitting on the lower, window aisle seat with a perfectly trimmed beard and moustache, dressed in black trousers, half-sweater, and a cream-coloured shirt with sleeves folded up, was going through the newspaper pages very attentively as if he wouldn't like to be disturbed even for a second. Sipping his tea, he scanned the newspaper as if he wanted to know each and every happening in the city, be it a minor episode in a local slum, a metro bulletin, or political hard news. While reading, he also glanced at the winter landscape outside the window and alternatively, the movements inside the train compartment—a lady getting up with her toothbrush and her husband still yawning out of laziness, a man setting his wet hairs by looking into the mirror, a boy listening to songs with his headphones on, and a man sitting on the upper berth informing his relative by phone that he was about to reach. All these happenings brought some sort of easiness into his eyes. The cold and fog were beginning to get on everyone's nerves. Passengers, with their sweaters already on, were looking out of their closed windowpanes, hoping for the sun to come out early and offer them some warmth and relief from the cold. But somehow, the cold did not seem to have much effect on that man, perhaps because he had completely dedicated his mind and soul to enjoying the view around him.

'So Mr. Iqbal, we are about to reach our destination?' said a middle-aged man who was sitting in front of him, interrupting his concentration.

'There is still 1 hour left,' said Iqbal, continuing with his unwavering attention outside the window. His way of answering soured the man's mood and withered the friendliness he was trying to grow. It highly disappointed him because Iqbal was the same man who a few hours ago enthusiastically talked about the great wars in history like the battle of Waterloo, the two world wars, and the brave battles fought by the Indian army. He even shared his own point of view by saying - A war is always fought between two strong and stubborn minds.

'You army men have a lot of patience,' said the man, folding his legs and disinterested in continuing the conversation further.

'Hmmm,' sighed Iqbal. 'You know me very well within just a few hours of interaction.'

The man simply acknowledged his answer this time with merely a snort and disdainful look. One hour passed and just 15 minutes were remaining for the Capital Express to reach the Delhi main station, its last stop. Iqbal turned his thoughts away from the window, gathered his bag and suitcase kept on the upper berth and started to pack his things. He went to the washroom to freshen up, then returned and picked up his luggage and walked towards the train door. He stood near the doorway, waiting for the train to enter the station. His eyes had a hypnotizing gaze; they were definitely searching for something, something very different. The wheels stopped rolling finally after reaching the Delhi main station. In the background could be heard the sound of the train announcement:

Train no. 14091 from Kanyakumari to New Delhi, Capital Express, has just arrived on Platform No. 1.

Iqbal gathered his luggage, ignoring the porter trying to persuade him to take his help and took a long walk towards the taxi stand.

He hailed a taxi and asked the driver, 'Chandni Chowk?'

'Get in,' said the driver.

He placed himself comfortably inside the taxi as the driver pushed the accelerator gently, steering the car into the busy Paharganj area. Paharganj is one of the three administrative subdivisions of the Central Delhi district. It is a thickly populated area due to its affordable hotels, lodges, restaurants, dhabas and a wide variety of shops.

'Sir, are you new to Delhi?' asked the taxi driver, who was a Punjabi.

'Yes.'

'Then it's certain that you will also fall in love with this city,' said the driver.

'Why is it like that?'

'Even I don't know, sir. Whoever comes here for the first time, they say that they are in love with this place and sometimes I hear people saying that they can even feel the air talking to them,' said the driver, laughing out loud with his big belly bouncing along.

'Indeed, there's something special about the air flowing here,' said Iqbal, sliding down the window of the front door. The crowd of moving vehicles and the busy streets gave him a strange happiness.

'How beautifully they are ignorant,' said Iqbal while the driver gave a double honk of the car horn. He turned towards the driver with a gentle smile on his face and said, 'Ignorance is bliss, my friend until it causes death.'

Curtain Raiser

I am Samarth, a resident of Old Delhi, more specifically Chandni Chowk, an extremely crowded area having a great symbolic significance in the history of India. For me, Delhi has always been a city where life is like a celebration, whether it's the lonely roads of the morning or it's the lively atmosphere of the night. Something or the other always happens here. Once, drifting off into some pleasant reveries, I stood under a streetlight alone and stared at the night sky. That was the time when I actually admired this city and pondered on the mysteries gifted to me, destiny being the biggest of them. Growing up as an orphan, clueless about my own origins, I always wondered—what is destiny? In the imagination of an adolescent boy, it was nothing but a glimmer of light at the end of a scary dark tunnel. But somewhere, I knew that destiny had a greater meaning. It had a spiritual value in everyone's life. Tired of searching for it, I surrendered to time and hoped it would give me a precise answer as the journey of life continued.

Years later, distances away from home, when I walked on one of the walkways of the Taj Mahal, it was still the same mystery that surprised me. A girl, admiring the monument of love, was walking beside me. My heart was heavy as I owed an apology to her. Though my simple apology could not compensate for her terrible loss, it would give me a sense of responsibility, for me to take care of her. But before I reveal her name, before I disclose my relationship with her, and before I tell you the meaning of destiny that I derived from that place, there's a story that you should know. A story that circles around my past, a story that defines my present, and a story that envisions my coming future.

It starts with two sisters, Aastha and Aradhna, both running an orphanage. Aastha was the elder sister who was tall and beautiful with blue-green eyes; her face portrayed her elegance, softness, inherent suppleness, patience, and perseverance. She was an ethereal beauty. The younger sister, Aradhna, was of medium height, with pretty brown eyes. She was a strict, candid, courageous, systematic, and focused woman. The difference in age between them was narrow.

They started the orphanage soon after their own life turned into a debacle. The sisters' parents died when they were completing their final years of graduation. If memory serves me right, the cause of their death was a road accident. Their loss was traumatic for the sisters and it took them a long time to recover from the shock. After coming to terms with their bereavement, both decided to remain together as they never wanted to taste those bitter days again. Both started working in a government office and earned a respectable salary. Nobody knows the exact reason why they suddenly chose the path of social work. But I could guess the reason. Maybe they wanted to share their love and warmth with children deprived of parental love and care, as they had already undergone similar pain.

Along with me, there were many children who lived in the orphanage with these angel-like sisters. Almost all of them were adopted by married couples who didn't have kids. But a time came when, including me, only eight children remained. No one came for adoption for almost two years. By that time, we had become so close to both the sisters that they decided to shut down the orphanage and move on to live like a family. Though we weren't related by blood nor had anything in common, our bond was so strong that no one could break it easily. Soon, the orphanage was closed, and we moved to Chandni Chowk for the beginning of a new life. Our new home was on the top floor of an old 3-storeyed building located in a congested street of Chawri Bazaar, the first wholesale market of Old Delhi that lies to the west of Jama Masjid. It is one of the main markets of Chandni Chowk and runs from the Red Fort to Fatehpuri Masjid. It has streets and homes that go back many centuries.

It had been almost two-and-a-half years since we'd been living a peaceful life there and the neighbourhood was very lively. The middle floor belonged to a busy man who rarely visited his home because he was always on some kind of a tour. Most often, I only saw a big lock hanging on his door. I didn't even know his first name. The ground floor belonged to the most happening married couple in the whole of Chandni Chowk, Mr. and Mrs. Desai. They always had plenty of time to fight with each other and not even a couple of seconds to share love. Mr. Jignesh Desai was a retired army man who loved only two things—his army gun, which he had with him to remember his proud days in service, and his black scooter, which he cleaned daily. He may have forgotten to brush his teeth in the morning but not to clean his scooter. The husband-wife's verbal fights attracted a strong viewership from the colony residents, any time of the day. Di always advised us to ignore them and we too obeyed her, even though it was intolerable.

When you finally emerge on to the streets, there is an identical 3-storeyed building facing ours, which has exactly the same façade and a long row of shops and houses on both sides.

Our home, a small and sweet home. It had a small kitchen from where we got our delicious nourishments, a hall with a TV and a dining table, two bedrooms, and one bathroom to the side of Di's bedroom. After a long and tiring search, our sisters were able to discover this particular building where we could find our perfect home. Like a perfect family, we sat together, ate together, and slept together. Each day that passed added a new chapter of happiness into our lives and each night that came showed us happy dreams of the next day. Everything was picture perfect.

But all this is now history. Those were the times when we all were kids. Now time has changed and so have we. The most disgusting habit that a human being develops is of jeopardizing one's own harmony. The sisters no longer hold each other's hand or stand united; rather, they stand at different corners like the two banks of a river. Some feud had cropped up between the two and now, they live separated from each other. The younger sister, Aradhna, along with the four girls—Avni, Tamanna, Sandhya, and Suhaani— live on the top floor of the building in front of ours. Luckily, when the fight took place between the two sisters, the family that lived on the top floor of that building had already moved out from there, as a result of which Aradhna Di did not need to go in search of a new house.

Speaking of the girls, Avni was beautiful, with her smiling face and semi-curly hair; she was sweet from her heart and lovely from her eyes—her simplicity was her attraction. Tamanna was a shy, little girl with brown skin and big eyes. She was a thoughtful girl and tolerant of emotional pain. Sandhya was the leading lady of the troop—she was fair, beautiful, fun loving, and bold. Suhaani was the most studious in the camp. She was sensible and empathetic.

I, along with Aarav, Mihir, and Youhaan lived with our elder sister, Aastha, in the old house. Aarav was a strong guy. A little short-tempered, he liked challenges, and had a lot of integrity and confidence. Youhaan was passionate, hardworking, and emotionally sensitive. Mihir was the joker in the pack of cards. Against the opinion of others, he believed he had a great sense of humour. He was very easy going, handsome, and rarely serious. Talking about me, apart from being judgemental about everything, I had never come across any other quality of me. I've been consistent in exploring more and more about myself, and it has never been a drawback. The process of discovery was more remarkable for me than the discovery itself.

Coming back to the sisters, both now hate to even look at each other's faces, so to see them talking is beyond imagination. They still work in the same office, but they are only concerned about their work, not about each other. Both sit in their respective cabins with their faces turned in opposite directions. They don't even like us boys and girls talking to each other and scold us whenever they find us talking through the Venetian windows of our respective bedrooms. The sisters never told us the reason behind their fight, and neither were we bothered or interested to know why. All I remember is their last conversation:

'So, it's finally over, Di?' asked Aradhna Di, standing at the doorstep with her luggage.

'I don't have the answer for that question, but if you think you'll be happy without me then I don't have the power to stop you.'

'I'll try my best to be happy without you.'

'You have the right to take decisions for your life.'

'Fine, but I have a request,' said Aradhna Di, dropping her bags and walking towards her elder sister. With a lot of expectations forcibly suppressed inside her, she continued, 'I'll take the girls with me and you will not say no to me, at least for our old time's sake.'

Aastha Di, after thinking for a long time, finally said, 'I'll not stop you.'

That was the end of it all, an end to the happy days, an end to the relationship between the two sisters, and the end of a perfect family. Fate has a habit of playing games, but the problem is that it always wins. The picture-perfect frame of our life just crashed to the ground and developed a big, deep crack.

I have still not revealed the small, romantic turnaround of my story, the love story that blossomed amongst us boys and the girls amidst all this turbulence. This fact was hidden from our sisters and we couldn't even think of the consequences if the secret were to be revealed. I know you may be thinking that we were not at an age to love like Romeo and Juliet, but to study like Einstein and Edison. But believe me, beautiful things happen by chance in life. We should never demean them by our ignorance and egocentric nature. For us, things had naturally fallen into place. The universe was eager to make us learn about love and the supreme feeling of falling into it. It wasn't easy. But after all, what fun would there have been if love didn't throw its own challenges?

We all pretended to ignore each other whenever our sisters were around or when they came to drop us at the bus stop in the morning. Both of them would stand at an appropriate distance between each other, with one looking east and the other looking west, and we would all stand in between them, desperately looking left and right at both of them. It was a relief when we heard the loud and weird horn of our bus. Once inside, we'd forget everything— the sisters, their fight and even our schoolmates sitting inside that vehicle. We only thought about each other. I always loved to sit near Avni and watch my brothers, Mihir sitting with Sandhya and Youhaan sitting along with Suhaani. There was one sight that always made me believe that the universe is not fair to everyone when it comes to love. Aarav and Tamanna sat on different seats. Like yet another tired cliché of an ordinary life, Tamanna loved Aarav deeply but Aarav didn't return her feelings. She liked him so much that she would watch him through her bedroom window, blushing. She would stare continuously at him in the classroom and then suddenly look the other way. In the temple, instead of seeking blessings for herself, she would pray for Aarav. As a young girl, she had strong desires locked in her heart for him and she lived in the hope of fulfilling them. Aarav always acted as if he was emotionless. He knew very well that Tamanna loved him secretly, but he paid no attention to her. I always prayed for Tamanna, that one day she may achieve her love.

Once our bus started moving, we were in a world of our own, like love birds flying freely in the blue sky, no matter what was happening on the earth. Inside the bus, our first and foremost task was to take out a fresh red rose from our inside blazer pocket (of course, excluding Aarav) and give it to the girls. They would take it with a hint of a smile and shyness on their pretty faces. We used to pick the roses from Aastha Di's terrace garden. She was very fond of gardening and we felt sorry for her because she would get to see her roses mostly on Sundays and other school holidays. On the way to our school, when our bus passed in front of India Gate, we four boys would stick our heads out of the bus window into the cold Delhi breeze and block the fast-blowing wind with our hands. A rush of immense ardour and dynamism would flow through our blood and veins. Gradually, this became a habit with us.

I sensed a delectation and thrill within me when my long hair would spread and fly behind my head in the hard-blowing, cold air. A feeling of euphoria raced within me in anticipation of arriving at my favourite place. That was my school—my garden, planted with fun.

The Premier School

The name written above was none other than our school's name. It was not one of Delhi's highly reputed and flourishing schools, it was only an average school loaded with students coming from different sections of society. Our poor sisters could only afford this on their moderate budget. But we never complained. We knew how difficult it must have been to take care of eight children's education, food, clothing, and other basic needs. We had high respect for them. But this respect was only in our minds, not in our actions, as the four of us went to school only to have fun!

We'd often stand and stare at our school's name and rack our brains, trying to figure out the meaning of the word 'Premier'. When we learned the importance of a dictionary, its meaning became clear. The word 'Premier' meant first in position or importance. When we came to know this, the four of us looked at each other's faces and burst out laughing, knowing that this word was applicable to none of us. But keeping aside these foolish thoughts, school was a place where I learned three important things—patience, perception, and creativity.

I learned patience from Mr. Shyam Rastogi, the principal of our school. Being a 50-year-old who believed in the Gandhian philosophy of truth and non-violence, he always used to advise the students about values and motivate them to walk the right path. I haven't seen a man more patient than him because he tolerated us. We four were known by the group name 'SAMY' inside the school premises. The name was developed by taking the first alphabet of each of our names and within a few years it became hugely popular. Within no time, it reached even the ears of our beloved principal. Our group was famous for its pranks and at the same time, infamous for academic performance. Our skills at planning and executing pranks led us to the principal's desk a number of times. Whenever we stood in his office room, I always felt like a hardcore criminal standing in the court, waiting for the judge's decision to be hanged. But the sad part was to see him getting blamed for the failure of addressing the indiscipline in school. People often called him weak, and in spite of that, I always saw him with a steady mind. He proved that patience indeed is the most potent weapon.

In Class 11, our student batch was divided into two different sections, Science and Commerce, and to add a little bit of flavour, Media & Mass Communication. It was like the history of the world, divided into B.C and A.D. We four belonged to the science group, along with the girls. We always loved to occupy the back benches, something that our teachers disapproved of. Out of the five subjects we studied, we hated four of them. English was our favourite period. It's not that we studied it seriously; it was the only period in which we got a chance to sleep. I was the exception to this—I never slept during the class. I'd just sit and stare at Avni, even though she never bothered to glance back. It was not because she disliked me, just that the words of our English teacher mattered to her more at that moment. And this is where I learned perception, from my English teacher, who sometimes took a different tangent while explaining the chapters in our syllabus.

'Hell,' said Narayan Sir in a stern voice. 'What is the definition of hell?'

Mr. Narayan Balakrishnan was our English teacher who was well known in the school for his strict and rigid style of teaching. During his teaching hours, he demanded only one thing from the students—discipline. Inspired strongly by Dante Alighieri's *Divine Comedy*, Narayan Sir continued with his apprehension of the world and the people in it.

'According to me, a man makes his own hell. Our drastic actions and unsolicited thoughts as living beings make the earth a living hell. Look around you, you'll see the seven sins and seven circles of hell everywhere, and we are so naive about it.'

'What the hell?' said Mihir, waking up from his peaceful sleep. 'He keeps saying this often,' he whispered, 'I think he's turning antisocial day by day.' Before I could say anything, a chalk piece came flying and hit Mihir's head. Narayan Sir had reached the edge of his patience, seeing his four special students enjoying a comfortable nap during his class every day. The three of them came out from their dream and also shook me out of my reverie.

'Hey, we are caught!' said Youhaan meekly to the three of us, which made me laugh deep inside my insane mind. Didn't the poor guy realise that the whole school, and even the principal, knew we slept at that time? Narayan Sir moved towards us in slow motion and our legs automatically began to straighten up thanks to the killing fear that began to grow within us. When his eyes went big with anger like the filmy villains of the 1980s, even the cleverest ones found their throats dry. But I don't know what happened to him on that day, he didn't scold us but told us to go and stand outside. We four went quietly outside the door without uttering a single word and stood there, enjoying nature's beauty. The cool breeze made Mihir do something crazy. He started to shine his watch on to Sandhya's face through the window. She got disturbed and looked towards the window. Soon her disturbance turned into calmness and she directed her beautiful smile towards Mihir. She was the first and the last human who could handle Mihir and his activities. Suddenly, the smile disappeared from her face and she looked towards the blackboard. Mihir couldn't understand exactly what had happened and he turned the other side. Standing there was Narayan Sir and the next sound I heard was that of a tight and strong slap on Mihir's cheeks. The sound of that slap echoed throughout the corridor and Mihir stood at his place. He slowly turned his head towards Narayan Sir. Tears began to roll down his face. Seeing him weeping like that, we began to laugh uncontrollably.

'What's happening here?' we heard a voice from behind. It was none other than our principal.

'Their old habit, creating a nuisance,' replied Narayan Sir.

'You four come to my room, I need to talk to you all,' ordered our principal and we almost became corpses. Very soon, we were about to enter our court room.

'What nonsense is this, Aarav?' our principal shouted angrily at Aarav. 'You hit that poor chap again?'

He was referring to a 2-day old incident where Aarav had had a small scuffle with Prithvi, the talented school topper. Like in every story, reel or real, my story also had a villain. A villain who serves as an obstacle the hero must overcome. It was Prithvi, and there was no specific reason for it. He shared the same classroom in which we breathed. The sight of him disgusted us; it was like an assault on our eyes.

'Dude, I think this man always lives in the past. I thought he will scold me,' said Mihir.

'Stand quiet,' I said.

'He is my best friend, sir, how could I hit him like that,' came the reply from Aarav, an unexpected one. We looked at him as if we'd got a high voltage shock. But we quickly realized it was just a trick he was playing to escape. Our principal looked like he was about to have a nervous breakdown after hearing that excuse!

Every student in the school corridor knew that we were born enemies. Prithvi was multi-talented, being the school topper, an excellent guitarist and good at literature. In straightforward words, he was talent personified. Maybe this was the hidden reason for our dislike.

He didn't have many friends in the school other than a mentally challenged girl who was very special for him. Her name was Radhika and he often met her when she came to the school with her mother and sister. She was suffering from mental retardation, a disorder appearing commonly before adulthood. People with mental retardation do not look like they have any type of disability; same was the case with Radhika, she looked like normal girls of her age and absolutely alright. Her disorder was a mild one. Her sister Meera was a student in our class and one of our very good friends. She often brought Radhika to the school during some cultural programmes, result days, and other important occasions. How Prithvi and Radhika became friends was unknown to me, but they were very close to each other.

Our principal took a deep breath and leaned forward with his reply. 'This is the last warning for you all, if I get one more complaint, you four are out from here. Now, get lost!'

After getting that alarming warning, we walked out of his room silent as lizards and inhaled some fresh oxygen, like prisoners getting bail after a long stay in prison. We decided to be a little careful now after getting that warning—we could not afford this issue to reach Aastha Di's ears as we didn't want to disappoint her and dash all her hopes.

Twenty minutes to go for lunch, and we were ravenously hungry. I was desperately waiting for the recess bell to ring when my eyes fell on Anjali Ma'am dancing on the stage with a group of students. Ms. Anjali Saxena taught dance in our school. She was a young lady of average height, fair, slim, beautiful, and a talented teacher. We all shared a close bond with her. She was like a butterfly, delicately spreading joy in my garden of fun. At this point in my story, she was engaged in choreographing a new dance for the annual function to be held in the school within a week. It is through her that I learned creativity.

'I was 13 years old when I had severely injured my right leg,' said Anjali ma'am, when she took her first-ever class in the school. 'The injury happened at such a time when I was preparing for a performance in my school. The doctor had advised me to take rest and not to use my injured leg much. But me being me...' she said, chuckling to herself.

'I applied a lot of brains and decided to perform a mute dance, you know the one where we mostly use our hands and upper body. It was a difficult one, but I cracked it. My performance was loved by the audience. I couldn't give up thinking that I had an injury.'

From her real-life example, I could explain to myself that creativity is not only about giving your best it's also about what you can deliver when you're at a loss.

After our tiresome school routine ended, we would straightaway dash into our school bus and quickly grab our favourite seats before the others reached. Usually, our energy would be lower than in the morning hours and so we did not mind taking a short nap till the bus reached our stop. Once we stepped out of the bus, it was the same old story—we boys and girls walking at a measured distance, faking animosity while feeling regret at having to ignore each other. It was a short walk from our bus stop through the cold streets before we reached our home. We had to walk through bustling crowds, past buildings packed with shops, sweet-sellers and other food vendors, and then past some houses and finally into our respective buildings.

'Hi sweethearts, how was your day?' asked Aastha Di with a cute smile on her innocent face.

'It was okay,' I replied with a clever smile on my wicked face. This was the usual conversation which always took place whenever we returned from school. But this was not the case in the building facing ours; Aradhna Di was a little strict with the girls and investigated them about their day by asking questions about complaints and assignments. The girls sometimes used to call her Lady Hitler whenever her scolding was intolerable. We felt so lucky that we were with Aastha Di who was so quiet, humble and lovely that she hated scolding us.

When we returned after our evening leisure, we would quickly take a bath and go downstairs, ready to visit the temple. This was our daily routine. The temple we visited daily was the Gauri Shankar Temple, one of the most important temples of Shaivism. The temple is dedicated to Lord Shiva and is blessed with an 800-year-old *lingam* which is universally known as the 'cosmic pillar' or the 'centre of the universe'. I loved the ambience of the place, and moreover, it taught me faith, something that I learned outside of my textbooks.

'Pandit Ji, tell me something about Lord Shiva,' I said to the temple priest, who was a middle-aged man ready to share his religious beliefs and knowledge to anyone who asked him. I loved to sit with him sometimes and learn about the things associated with our origin and existence.

'Everybody knows that he's the third god in the Hindu triumvirate,' said the priest, cutting out a piece of coconut for me. 'Our imperfect world needs a powerful God like him, who can destruct and recreate it when the power of evil becomes relentless. Shiva the Destroyer will always save us and show us the way to redemption.'

'Is destruction an absolute necessity and the only way to save this world?' I asked, chewing the coconut.

'Are you scared?' asked the priest laughingly. 'It's okay if you're scared because one should be about one's deeds and their outcomes.'

I still had not achieved that level of maturity where I could've related his answer to my question. As a patient boy, I waited for him to speak more and clear my confusion.

'What exactly is this world?' he continued to enlighten me. 'It's not just matter and energy; it's also the result of our actions and deeds. If you see a beggar begging in the corner of a street, it's because the employment rate is not favourable enough to offer him a job. The low employment rate can be because of the slow economic growth or maybe due to the beggar's own action, because he never invested time in upskilling or educating himself.'

The priest stood up and started to walk in the temple premises along with me. I was slowly getting aligned to his thoughts and eventually towards the answer I was looking for.

'The slowness in economic growth,' continued the priest, 'can be again because of multiple reasons—financial sectors in a mess or low income for the farmers. This long chain will continue, and it isn't straightforward to trace it back to the roots. In the end, whatever we do will result in something good or evil. It's our primary responsibility to contribute more towards goodness and lessen the weight of evil.'

'And lesser the evil means more are the chances of saving the world from destruction.'

'Well, no human can guarantee that. All I can say is you got the point that I was trying to convey.'

I was a little disappointed. That incomplete answer irritated me like an irritant substance causing discomfort in my body. Why can't some questions be answered with a simple yes or no, I thought.

'Is it wrong to say that being good also asks us to live under certain rules and regulations?' I asked, trying to create a spinoff from my original query.

'You're absolutely right, and I don't see a problem in living with rules.'

'I don't agree with that,' I said, opposing him probably for the first time in my life. 'Rules restrict me, and I want to live a free life.'

The priest looked at his watch and realized that it was time for the evening prayer. Before leaving my pot of understanding unfilled, he decided to cover it with a lid of mystery.

'I don't think I can make you believe immediately that rules are important for a society,' said the priest, walking back inside the temple. 'But listen to this—Lord Ram had to abandon Mata Sita in the forest after their return to Ayodhya. Though this decision of Lord Ram is still open to criticism in modern times, he did it for the wellbeing of society. Howsoever foolish the subjects of his kingdom, he thought like an ideal king devoted to dharma, and not as a husband. When God himself gave primary importance to the welfare of the society, then who are we, mere humans, to not accept this?'

The priest concluded his teachings for the day. He then began with the preparations of the evening prayer, answering the wait of all the devotees. I was left behind in that crowd with my own thoughts screwing up my mind. There is not a single person alive who knows what his dharma is, I thought. I could've bet on that. What difference would it make if I lived a disciplined life? Nothing. There was only one thing in this world today that ensured a happy living—selfishness. Time, of course, proved me wrong later.

The Start of Preparations

The whole school was enveloped in an atmosphere of celebration and busy with preparations for the annual day. Everybody was busy with their own programmes and activities. Some were engaged in the stage decoration, helping the craftsmen, some were running behind teachers with the list of programmes, and some were practicing with their groups. The teachers of the cultural committee were busy scheduling the programme items. They were selecting students for participation in various items and hiring some of them for help. The students involved in the cultural committee were busy preparing duty charts, duty assignments, and arrangements. The whole atmosphere was so filled with excitement and enthusiasm that we felt compelled to put on our dancing shoes and join Anjali Ma'am's dance troupe. We entered the audition room where Ma'am was selecting the students for her dance. The level of excitement was clearly visible on our flushed faces. But soon, our excitement meter dropped to zero when we saw Prithvi sitting on a chair inside the audition room. He was with his guitar, playing his chords and singing a particular song, one I'd heard him sing often during the past one year. It was a self-composed song and he would sing it at every opportunity. I couldn't understand why this creature always showed up wherever we went.

'He is taking auditions for singing,' said Aarav.

'And we are giving auditions here; that's disgusting,' I replied.

We could do nothing, nor could we order him to leave, because we didn't have the right to do so and we did not want to create any commotion while Miss Anjali was taking the auditions.

'All right students, line up fast and no talking, please,' said Ma'am.

One by one, each student went up to give their best. Some were good, some were horrible, and some were stupendous. When our chance came, we gave our best and Ma'am was very impressed by us. At once, she placed our names at the top of her list.

'I hope Sandhya and the girls will also be selected,' said Mihir and his wish came true very soon. The girls were also selected, making a dance group of about 30 students. On the other side, Prithvi's selection process was also progressing.

'Is your work over?' shouted Prithvi towards Anjali Ma'am, giving a gentle smile.

'Almost,' she shouted, smiling back.

That irritated us very much. Each and everything he did irritated us, it sucked our blood out and replaced it with poison.

The same day, after school in the evening, we were sitting on the terrace wall looking curiously towards the window of the front building. Aarav didn't join us; he was busy with watering the plants as Aastha Di had made him the caretaker of her terrace garden. I didn't realize when my mind got diverted from the window to the evening because that evening was something different. It was silent, still, calm and cold, flashing a pale yellow light onto my eyes. The setting sun's red rays lit up the sky above the western horizon, signalling a flight of birds to return to their nests. It was like someone had painted us on a paper. When I looked around for a moment, I saw that Mihir too was enjoying nature's masterpiece. Mihir and I were completely mesmerized by this view, but Youhaan wasn't because he was still looking towards the window to get a small glimpse of Suhaani. Her face was more special for him than any beautiful scene. We both decided to help Aarav with his work and left Youhaan alone to enjoy the evening in his own way. When we finished our work within a few minutes, we saw Youhaan giving an enigmatic smile like the Mona Lisa. But the secret behind this smile was clear, as Suhaani was standing at the window.

'Youhaan!' shouted Mihir loudly into his ears, just to disturb him, after which he started laughing. Youhaan angrily pushed him, which caused the clay pot to slip from Mihir's hands down to the ground. We watched the pot falling down till it crashed on to Desai Uncle's scooter, breaking its mirror completely. The front part of the scooter became dirty with mud and got scratched.

'Miiiihhiiiirrrr!' came a loud shout from the ground floor. It was a familiar voice, filled with anger, annoyance, and displeasure, bringing alive the legendary enmity between Desai Uncle and Mihir. Their enmity had an interesting backstory. It was a year ago when, one evening, it was raining heavily all over Delhi.

Mihir decided to convey his feelings to Sandhya. But the problem he faced was how to reach the place where she was waiting for him. He decided to borrow Desai Uncle's scooter without asking him and smartly took it away while it was kept out in the rain. Perhaps, Desai Uncle had forgotten to lock it? Mihir drove the scooter through the streets of Chandni Chowk and finally reached in front of Moti Cinema, where Sandhya was waiting for him. She was holding a blue umbrella with white circles on it and wearing a plain white top and blue jeans with trendy, white Doc Martens. She looked like a fairy standing in the rain. Mihir parked the scooter by the side of the road and slowly started walking towards her. With each step he placed forward her smile got broader and broader. Mihir was full of confidence. He came close to her and took out a piece of paper from his pocket.

'I've prepared something for you,' said Mihir, unfolding the paper and clearing his throat. 'People talk about the moon and stars,' he started reading it, 'but I say the way you illuminate the darkness in my life, your light is more powerful than theirs. This also reminds me of an interesting thought I had the other day. I imagined you and me living up to an age where technology has become so efficient that it has made life possible after death. I was fascinated by this and thought to share it with you. How beautiful it would be to live rationally till eternity, you and me till the end of time.'

After listening to his words, Sandhya started laughing. 'This is not how you propose a girl Mihir,' she said.

'Wasn't it good,' asked Mihir, confused.

'It looked like you prepared for a speech competition,' she said, laughing uncontrollably. Sandhya controlled her laughter and slowly started walking towards him. 'You could've simply said...'

Before she could finish, Mihir, with shock on his face shouted, 'My scooter!' and started running to the place where it was parked. He saw his scooter being picked up by the traffic police.

'That's my scooter, sir,' shouted Mihir and went running towards the policeman.

'Mihir, stop!'

'Sir, I am so sorry, sir!' cried Mihir.

'Your scooter was parked in the no-parking zone,' said the inspector.

'Sir, it happened by mistake, I didn't notice the 'No Parking' board.'

'Sir, we are so sorry,' said Sandhya, recognizing the scooter. She realized what consequences he has to bear if this mistake was not rectified. 'He will not repeat this. Yes, Mihir?' she said and turned towards him. Mihir nodded his head but it was too late.

'Listen guys, I can do nothing,' said the inspector. 'You need to come to the area police station, pay the penalty and take the vehicle.' The inspector went off, leaving Mihir in tears. He saw Desai Uncle's scooter being mercilessly hauled away by the traffic police.

'Mihir, I am really very upset because of you. You've spoiled our evening,' said Sandhya and she started walking.

'Stop, Sandhya, for my sake, please!' said Mihir and he caught hold of her hand. He slowly came close to her and stared deeply into her eyes. They started walking down the lane, under the rainclouds, sharing one umbrella.

'Do you love me?' asked Mihir. At that moment, the eighth wonder of the world happened. Mihir became serious. 'If yes, *just say it and I will replace all your worries, sadness, and tensions with just their opposites.'*

His words brought back Sandhya's beautiful smile. And that was it, the start of a cute and charming relationship. When he returned home, he quietly pasted a note on Desai Uncle's door on which was written:

Please take your scooter from the nearby police station and pay the penalty.

Yours sincerely

Mihir

And soon, we heard a loud roar from the ground floor, 'Miiiihhiiiirrrr!' When everyone approached him to ask the reason for taking the scooter, he said, 'I just wanted to take a ride, that's all,' and escaped.

But that was the start of it all, the start of an unwanted enmity between Mihir and Desai Uncle. Desai Uncle considered Mihir as a parasite ready to eat up his life. Sometimes, he saw frightening nightmares about his scooter being destroyed by the demon who lived upstairs. But also, he was kind enough to make him understand the importance of trust and valuing other's property.

'One day, I met an Arab,' said Desai Uncle, riding his scooter back home from the police station on the same day. Mihir was sitting behind him, listening to the most valuable piece of advice he could ever get.

'He told me a story when he was on a shopping spree around Dubai's famous markets. He had an acquaintance beside him who he didn't know was a professional thief. The Arab handed over his suitcase containing valuable belongings to him and entered into a diamond showroom. The store manager was a vigilant man who immediately recognized the acquaintance standing outside.'

Desai Uncle took a left turn while Mihir, who was hooked on the story, tapped him on his shoulder and said, 'Uncle, tell me more.'

'The Arab ran outside the shop when he got to know the true identity of the man who accompanied him. Worried about his expensive belongings, he wanted to confront the man and get him arrested. But the thief was nowhere to be seen. The Arab could only find his suitcase safely kept on the ground with a note on the top.'

It was night when they finally reached home. The night was cold and dark, with the sky swept clean of clouds. Mihir's curiosity was burning inside him, enough to keep him warm.

'What was written on the note?' he asked, excitingly.

'The Arab couldn't believe what was written on it,' said Desai Uncle, parking his scooter under the parking shed. 'The thief wrote: I would've run away with this long before, but the trust you placed in me will follow me everywhere. Surprisingly, I realized that I'm a thief by choice, not by nature.'

Desai Uncle stood at his doorstep and said one last thing before entering inside. 'Always remember Mihir, that whatever you choose might not come as a perfect decision every time. It's okay to be wrong, but it's a sin to consider it as your place of comfort.'

As Desai Uncle closed the door behind him, Mihir entered into a state of realization, not one that could transform him immediately but the one that would prick him often. He would always carry it as a burning torch to enlighten his faith.

A Crossover with Fate

'Twist your body properly,' said Anjali Ma'am, while she was demonstrating the dance steps to us.

It felt very good to be practicing in the open air on the stage, listening to the chirping of birds and inhaling fresh oxygen. Ma'am not only taught us the steps, but she also taught us the importance of dance. She told us that dance is a form of expression, social interaction and exercise. Dance should be taken seriously as it is an art that teaches us to express oneself fully and also initiates a sense of unity.

'Properly Mihir, you are missing the beats,' said Ma'am, correcting Mihir. She was a thorough professional and a whole-hearted perfectionist. She was giving every bit of her effort to make our dance the highlight of the show. The whole group gave quite a good start to the dance and Ma'am was happy with our initial stage efforts. When the practice was over for the day, she bought fresh hot samosas as refreshments for everyone. While we were enjoying the tasty samosas, she started telling us about Michael Jackson, how he was an inspiration for her, and how she worshipped him as her idol.

'He was more than a King of Pop or the master of moonwalking for me,' said Anjali Ma'am, sitting in front of us. 'You know, his father Joseph Jackson started a musical group known as the Jackson 5 whose members were none other than his offspring. MJ was five years old when his father made him a member of the group. They build up a strong following by playing local gigs and countless struggles. If I remember correctly, it was in 1969 when Jackson 5 was finally introduced to the music world.'

We learned something new that day. Apart from his chart-topping songs, Michael Jackson's best performance also included his own life, which was inspirational and riveting.

'When Michael Jackson launched his solo career,' continued Ma'am, 'he became an instant pop sensation, and his album topped the musical charts. And he achieved all that at the age of 13. Can you imagine that?'

We could've never imagined that. And no one should've expected that from us in the first place. At the age of 13, we were rummaging through the streets of Delhi in search of our own identity. Who gave birth to us? Where did we belong? A few years of our childhood were exhausted by these fundamental questions.

'It doesn't matter at what age he achieved success,' said Ma'am, standing up and walking around us. 'What's important is at what age he started working towards his goals. You all will soon step out of these school gates and trust me, the world is a harsh place to survive. The only way to face it is by being clear about your goals and setting up a concrete path to success.'

Her words really set us thinking. When I looked back to all the bygone years, I couldn't remember anything that could be termed as success or merit. I couldn't believe it because all I had was numerous warnings for indiscipline and the embarrassing moments that I had to face in front of my family.

'It will be a two-hour practice every day as we did today,' said Anjali Ma'am, bringing me out of my shameful memories. 'We will begin the practice sharp at 8:00 am tomorrow and everybody should be on time.'

'Well, I don't mind coming daily for a tasty samosa,' said Mihir.

We all said 'Yes!' in unison and nodded our heads to show our approval while she piled up her things and stood up to leave. When we were coming down from the stage, we saw Prithvi crossing by the side. Aarav was just waiting for this precious opportunity. After everybody had left— especially the girls, who disapproved of us fighting with others—the four of us went and stopped Prithvi in his tracks.

'Keep away from us, chap,' said Aarav in a strong voice with his hands on Prithvi's shoulder. Prithvi didn't reply anything, rather he just removed Aarav's hand from his shoulder and started walking again. His attitude further increased Aarav's adrenalin level and he was about to use his hands on Prithvi when I stopped him. I'd had enough of this, especially after learning about great men who achieved glory when they were my age.

Aarav controlled himself, blocked him again, and said, 'You should not be seen talking with Anjali Ma'am anymore. Do you get that?' Prithvi again didn't reply anything and just ignored us. We too thought it wouldn't be wise to talk to him too much as he could go and complain against us to the principal.

In the evening, around 7:30 pm, we were all getting ready to go to the temple. I quickly got dressed and reached downstairs, where I heard some loud shouting around me. When I turned back, I saw Mihir already peeping inside

Desai Uncle's window. I reached him, caught hold of his shirt and asked him, 'What the hell are you doing?'

'You can also join me, it's too much fun.'

I obeyed his words and peeped inside the window and saw Desai Aunty shouting at her husband, saying:

'I am fed up of this man.'

'If you are fed up of me, then why do you look at my face again and again?' shouted Desai Uncle at the top of his voice.

'It's my fate since we are living under one roof.'

'Get down, both of you,' shouted Di from behind us and we both got off quickly.

'What were you both doing? I had told you to ignore them,' said Di with a little anger on her face. At that moment, we heard a loud shout from inside the window. It was Aunty and she sounded tense. We quickly entered inside Desai Uncle's house and saw him tumbled on the floor, holding his chest.

'What happened to him?' asked Di, running towards him quickly.

'I don't know, he was shouting at me and suddenly...' said Aunty, crying out.

'He's sweating heavily, I think it may be a heart attack. Let me call the ambulance,' said Mihir quickly, reaching the telephone and dialling the emergency number.

The ambulance took some time to reach the address and very soon, Desai Uncle was rushed to the nearby hospital. Aradhna Di and the girls were watching these developments from their window. Aastha Di accompanied Aunty in the ambulance; we four followed by auto and reached the hospital quickly. As the auto driver applied the brakes, Mihir stepped out and started running towards the doors of the hospital. We followed him after paying the driver. By the time we reached, Uncle was already admitted in the I.C.U.

'What did the doctor say?' asked Mihir. 'Is he alright?'

'He is in the I.C.U.' said Di, consoling Aunty who was crying beside her. 'The doctors are preparing for the ECG and can say anything post the results only.'

I saw Uncle hooked up with a heart monitor and an oxygen mask to relax his heart. It must have been very painful for Aunty to see her husband in this condition. In spite of all the irrelevant fights that happened between them, it was the bond of marriage that came out stronger. But it was Mihir who surprised me the most. His reaction was totally unexpected. Maybe it was respect for Desai Uncle that was making him do this. Unprecedentedly, Mihir taught me something that day—the importance of a family. Family meant home. Tried and tested, when life allows you to go back home one day, you should have people around you to celebrate and break bread with. We all were a family. Though stitched, yet together.

The next day at school was very tiring for us as we had to put in extra efforts for the annual day function. Anjali Ma'am insisted on practicing with extra energy. We were a bit reluctant because of our late-night stay in the hospital and could doze literally anywhere. Suddenly, our school cultural coordinator, Ramesh, came into our practice area to make an announcement. He announced that a competition was to be held among students on 'World's Amazing Facts' during the annual function and that interested students should give their names to their respective class teachers. We were sure that Prithvi would definitely participate in this and this was the chance to beat him. It felt more respectful to be involved in a competitive fight.

When we reached home that day, we quickly had our lunch and straightaway rushed to the internet cafe to research the unheard facts of the globe. We didn't want to miss even a small fact which could lead us to winning the competition. After searching a few sites, we collected a good number of facts which was quite enough, and the only thing left was to select the best among them and arrange them in order. When we came out of the café, we were quite satisfied with our work and were jumping on the streets with joy. By mistake, Youhaan collided with a man on the street and fell down on the pavement. Luckily, he didn't get hurt and stood up slowly, while looking at the man who seemed to be a little annoyed.

'I am sorry,' said Youhaan.

'It's ok,' replied the man, cooling down. He collected his two books which had fallen to the ground. The man was wearing a light blue shirt with black trousers and a black-coloured coat. He had short hair, trimmed moustache, and beard.

'Hi, my name is Iqbal,' he said, extending his hand for a handshake. 'I live here in Chandni Chowk.'

'I am Youhaan and these are my brothers Samarth, Aarav and Mihir. We also live in Chandni Chowk.'

'Oh! That's good and nice to meet you all. I am little busy and running out of time, so see you later,' said the man and he walked away. We all looked at him curiously till he disappeared in the crowd. My intuitions were never right, but they were stronger this time. They made me believe that we'll meet that man again. There was something in him that made it hard for me to ignore this 'accidental' meeting. He was not meant to collide with us like that and then blend with the crowd. Some strangers derive a more significant meaning out of your life than your close ones.

Late at night, the four of us discussed our competition and tried to convince Aarav to participate in it. 'You can easily beat him, brother, there's no element of doubt in it,' said Youhaan in an appealing way. 'He is nothing in front of you.'

'Just think, if you win this one, you could easily impress our principal and he will surely have praises for you,' said I, in support. That was the only confidence booster he needed, and it seemed to inject energy into his veins.

'Tamanna will also be happy if you win,' said Mihir.

'Shut up Mihir,' replied Aarav, as if the name Tamanna meant nothing to him. 'I am ready, you all just wait and see.'

Next morning at the breakfast table, we three were having our breakfast in the usual way, relishing the food and eating heartily. Only Aarav's face was a bit serious. He was eating the bread with a very determined look on his face; it seemed like he was thinking of something very deeply.

'I will not allow him to win this time,' Aarav spoke out suddenly and the words were like a thunderbolt. We didn't say a single word and stayed quiet as squirrels. 'I will throw a strong reply to his face and laugh out loud, so that everyone will hear it,'

'Your bags are ready and be fast,' ordered Di.

We finished our breakfast and rushed downstairs to wait for Di as she usually took about five minutes to come down.

'Hey Aarav, look up—who's watching you?' said Mihir and when we looked up, we saw Tamanna casting her most precious smile only for Aarav. He stared her fixedly for a minute and then turned his head away. Martin Luther King Jr. once said, 'Nothing in the world is more dangerous than sincere ignorance and conscientious stupidity.' These words perfectly applied to Aarav's behaviour towards Tamanna. My hopes of seeing them both together were sinking because of this.

When we reached school, we had some time left for the practice to begin. I rushed towards the notice board to check the list of programmes. There was a little crowd that was gathered near the notice board and I somehow managed to reach the front. There were many lists on the notice board, including the final programmes list and the names of students participating in each program. When I came out of the crowd, I said to Mihir and Youhaan, 'Prithvi has given his name for the competition.'

'Hey guys,' we heard someone shouting from behind us. When we turned back, we saw Aarav running towards us. 'I gave my name too,' said Aarav, breathing a little fast.

'Great job, bro!' said Youhaan.

'I also have good news,' I said to them smilingly. 'Our dance show is selected for the finale.'

Everyone was happy to hear that. It felt nice to see things going in our way for the time being. We left that place, continuing our talk. We got into the rehearsal area and started practicing along with Anjali Ma'am.

In the evening, we were again in the hospital to inspect Desai Uncle's condition. He was shifted into another room from the I.C.U., which meant that his condition was now normal. That news was really like the fresh smell of wet soil. When we entered the room, we saw Aradhna Di already standing there, along with the girls. Both the sisters made eye contact for a few seconds and then looked away. I saw the doctor running his pen on the notepad, writing down the required medicine.

'These are some medicines that you must bring immediately,' said the doctor, handing over the slip to Aradhna Di.

'Now, how is he, Doctor?' asked Aastha Di.

'Well, it was just a minor attack, nothing to fear as such,' replied the doctor. 'Take care that he has his medicines on time and follows a heart-healthy diet. He can go home within a few days.'

'Thank God,' said Di.

'It seems that he is under a lot of stress. Is he tense over something that he spends a lot of time thinking about?' asked the doctor. As soon as he asked this question, each and every person standing in that room, including

Desai Uncle, turned their head towards Mihir. To divert everyone's attention, Mihir snatched the bag of apples from Sandhya's hand and walked towards Desai Uncle.

'Uncle, I brought apples for you,' said Mihir with a smile.

The Annual Day Function

The days passed, rehearsals were over, and preparations finished. The celebrations began and expectations rose...our annual day was here, the day most awaited. I was nervous. The last time I was this nervous about something was when I had been caught cheating in the examination. I thought I would be rusticated that day itself, but thankfully it all ended with some thoughtful advice. Fear sometimes reminds you of your worst memories. I still remember what my principal told me that day.

'He needs some guidance,' he said, looking at Aastha Di. 'I'm sure you'll make him understand the qualities of a literate person.' He then turned towards me and said, 'The path to absolute truth passes through rough terrain, but it's reliable. You'll feel at peace. If you always tend to find a clever route, most likely, you'll end at the wrong place.'

I might have needed another life to understand his words then, but his intentions were clear. It may have been the power of his words that I never attempted to cheat in my exams after that.

'Please wear your dance costumes as just one hour is left for the start,' said Avni, seeing me lost in my thoughts and fiddling around the school.

'Yes of course,' I said with an embarrassed smile. 'I was just thinking about Aarav's competition.'

'He applied for it in spite of knowing that Prithvi will be participating?'

Her question was a good one but the sound of the name 'Prithvi' was irritating.

'Yes, and that shows his courage,' I responded, on Aarav's behalf. 'Soon, Prithvi will be sitting in the loser's seat.'

'Okay relax,' she said, placing her hands on my shoulders. 'Why don't we all go for a walk around the school together?' asked Avni.

I liked her suggestion and quickly got into my dance costume. We went around the corridors, looking at the different activities happening around us. We saw Narayan Sir scolding Amit for not being serious about his welcome speech, and the peon carrying a tray of trophies for the meritorious and victorious students.

'Another honour for that crap,' said Aarav disrespectfully, referring to Prithvi.

We could see participants of different programmes checking their costumes and accessories, the stage decorators indulging in some serious art work, electricians testing mikes and lighting arrangements, volunteers making the chair arrangements, students and teachers giving a final touch to their programs. When we came out into the open air, we saw Prithvi helping his parents to their chairs. He was also helping Meera, Radhika and their parents to get a satisfactory seating arrangement. I took a look at my watch and it showed 6:45 pm. Just 15 minutes were left for the beginning of the show. The moon was shining lightly against the dark backdrop of the sky and a cold breeze was beginning to blow.

'I've been looking for you people all around the school premises,' shouted Anjali Ma'am angrily, walking rapidly towards us. 'This is intolerable I want you all in the classrooms at this very minute.'

'Ma'am we were...' began Tamanna, but Ma'am cut her short. 'No explanations required, just be quick.' Before she could get more annoyed, we ran quickly towards the classroom.

Our classroom was on the left side of the stage, giving a clear view of all the happenings on stage and among the crowd. It was 7:15 pm and we could see the parents, staff members, teachers, and our principal already at their seats and awaiting the grand opening ceremony. The lighting arrangement was fabulous; no doubt it was going to be the highlight of the function. It was clear that our principal had put in a lot of money this time and certainly he must have gone over budget. I saw Aastha and Aradhna Di had already occupied their seats, sitting adjacent to each other. There was a narrow aisle in between them for the students and teachers to reach upstairs. I wondered how this miracle happened and pointed it out to others as well. I was lucky to have seen it. After a long time, we saw them both together but still divided by a narrow boundary. I hoped the gap would be closed soon. Just then, the two anchors appeared on stage, shouting in unison:

Good evening to one and all, welcome to the 25th annual day celebration of Premier School.

Against the waves of applause breaking out, it struck me that this was our school's silver jubilee celebration. Of course, that was the reason Mr. Rastogi had spared no expense!

When I refocused my attention towards the stage, I heard the anchors inviting the teachers and principal for the lighting of the lamp. Within minutes, the lamp was spreading the grace of God in the darkness, followed by the prayer song sung by our teachers.

A perfect start for the evening.

'With the blessings of God, now we begin this festive evening. Firstly, I call upon Amit to make his welcome address. Following this will be a performance by the tiny wonders of the KG section.'

As every performance graced the stage, the appreciation from the audience increased, the sound of clapping grew louder, instilling confidence among the students. But the atmosphere inside the classroom was tensed.

'I am very sure that you are going to rock,' said Tamanna, gazing deeply into Aarav's eyes.

'Thank you for that,' replied Aarav in an unenthusiastic manner. Nevertheless, after that reply, Tamanna's smile lingered. She still had courage and confidence in her love that one day Aarav would be with her.

I looked at my watch, and it showed 8:45 pm. 'I think it's time, Aarav. You should be ready,' I said, looking back at him.

'Yes, I am just calming my nerves,' said Aarav. 'I'm sensing a little stage fright.'

Coming up next is a competition for our 12th standard students. It's called 'World's Amazing Facts'; the student with the best facts will be awarded the first prize and will be honoured at the end of the program.

My heartbeat started to race faster as the anchors called upon the names one by one. There were eight contestants participating in the contest and they lined up in order on the stage as their names were called out. I could sense the nervousness which those students were feeling standing on the stage, especially when they had a strong competitor like Prithvi. But I was more concerned about Aarav; he had to give his best to win this and I prayed that the facts which we had collected should grab the audience's attention and make them wonder.

The first contestant we have is Nikhil Upadhyay.

Nikhil appeared on stage and his facts were just average, as I'd heard them somewhere, sometime. I was confident that our facts were far better than his, but still, presentation mattered. I was hoping Aarav's nervousness had settled down. I felt like going on the stage to reassure him, and tell him to be brave and breathe easy. One by one, the names were called and with each performance, Aarav's turn was nearing. Finally, I heard it.

The Competitive Streak

Now, I may call upon Aarav to present his facts before us. Aarav slowly walked towards the front of the stage and the spotlights above focused upon him, leaving the rest of the stage in darkness. I crossed my fingers as he held his mike. I could see the expectations and worry on the face of my friends, with each wishing him good luck in their hearts. In the silence, Aarav started to speak:

'A hearty good evening to all of you. I hope you all are enjoying this wonderful evening. I Aarav, am here to make your evening a little more interesting.'

He was fidgeting a bit out of nervousness but managed to keep the momentum going. 'As I am a student of science, I take the privilege to reveal firstly, some facts related to science that you may not know. Most of us like to add garlic in our food, but have any of you tasted it with your foot? Sounds crazy, but it's true. If you rub garlic on your foot then within half an hour, you'll be able to taste it because it travels through your bloodstream!'

As I continued listening him, I remembered the days when we lived in the orphanage. We used to stand in front of everyone and speak five lines about ourselves. The sisters thought ahead of time, they insisted on our learning the art of public speaking. Being orphans, they feared we might have to seek encouragement to voice our opinions when we grow up. Aastha Di would be proud of Aarav, I thought, remembering those old days.

'Every one of you must have heard about the planet Neptune,' continued Aarav, 'but there is something you may not know about its discovery, which is still a controversy. You'll be wondering what I mean if I say Neptune came into existence through mathematics instead of science. Galileo was the first person to see it, but he ignored it, considering it a star, not as a planet. Later, French and English mathematicians predicted that a new planet would be discovered in a specific region of the sky. And till date, astronomers battle over who made the actual discovery—isn't it strange?'

The audience reacted towards the first few facts with a loud round of applause and seeing it, I said to myself, 'Good going, dude.'

'I am sure all of you know how a tiger looks, isn't it? But how many of you know how a *Liger* looks?' said Aarav this time taming his nervousness. There were some murmuring sounds in the audience, but he soon cleared the confusion.

'Don't worry, I'll tell you. Liger is the largest of all known cat species and represents a hybrid cross between a male lion and a female tiger. The same is the case of the *Tiglon,* a hybrid cross of female lion and male tiger. Nature has still many wonders to unfold, my dear friends.' *(Applause).*

'The next one might be unfamiliar to many of you—the existence of a parallel universe. Now what is a parallel universe? It's a universe that exists alongside ours, and which may possess different physical laws or a different history. Just imagine there may be a clone of you who is living in a different parallel universe and doing the same things which you are doing but with different outcomes!'

'The next fact is related to our beautiful trees. How much do all of you know about the trees around us? If you don't know much, then increase your knowledge with this one. *Nepenthes rajah* in Mount Kinabalu, the Madagascar tree in South Africa, and Ya-te-veo in Central America are a few examples of carnivorous trees. Next time you pluck a leaf, check out the tree first.' *(Audience laughs and then claps)*

With this, Aarav completed his presentation. Suddenly the silence in the audience broke and I could only hear the sound of clapping around me. I exhaled a deep breath of satisfaction and experienced a new joy running within me. My brothers were thrilled too, they were shouting out loud, expressing their uncontrollable happiness. Tamanna was emotional, seeing Aarav being appreciated. I wished I could see Aastha Di at this moment, but she was not visible in the dark among the audience. I hoped she was enjoying this moment too.

'You've done it brother,' I said to myself. This, I thought, would be a shock for some people in the school like our principal, Prithvi, Narayan Sir and the rest of the teachers who considered SAMY as zeroes. But my concentration returned to the stage when the anchors announced the next name.

The next and the final participant—please welcome Prithvi Mathur.

'Luck should not be with him this time,' said Youhaan, as Prithvi appeared on the stage. Placing my palm on my heart, I prayed Youhaan's words would come true. The audience grew silent and words started to pour out of his mouth.

'Namaste to my wonderful audience,' said Prithvi, starting with. 'I am here to reveal some facts which will need only 10 minutes out of your precious time and I promise you'll never forget it. Since we all are born in India, we often boast that we are aware of every fact about our country. I've brought some facts related to our country and I hope to surprise you all.'

Prithvi was neither stepping back and forth nor were his hands sweaty and cold with stage fright. He already had years of practice in addressing such a huge audience.

'We all love to play snakes and ladders, isn't it?' asked Prithvi. 'But in Indian history, it was something else. The game 'Snakes and Ladders' was created by the 13th century poet saint Gyandev. It was originally called *'Mokshpaat'*. The ladders in the game represented virtues and the snakes indicated vices. As time passed, the game underwent several changes, but the meaning remained the same—that good deeds take us to heaven and evil to a cycle of rebirths. Now when we play in this modern age, do we think of these things? Of course not, we simply give it to our little ones to have fun.' *(Loud round of applause)*

'It's a common fact that the earth takes 365 days to orbit the sun but who calculated it? Bhaskaracharya, in the 5th century, calculated the time taken by the earth to orbit the sun before any other astronomer. He calculated the exact time which is 365.258756484 days. Aren't we proud of our ancestors?

The next fact I am about to unveil concerns Indian coins, which is still unknown to many. Isn't it strange? We use these coins in our daily life and yet, we are unaware of some facts related to them. Anyway, I was about to tell you that Indian coins are mainly produced in four cities—Delhi, Mumbai, Hyderabad and Kolkata. Each city puts an identification mark or a mint mark under the year of issue—Delhi has a dot, Mumbai has a diamond, Hyderabad has a star and Kolkata has nothing beneath the year. Now, the next time you see a coin, look for this!'

Coins...they transitioned me again to a different time from that classroom. While living in the orphanage, Aradhna Di used to play a game with us where she hid coins and divided us into groups to find it. Each group pretended to be families who've lost a valuable amount of money in a heist. They must now set out on an expedition to retrieve what they've lost. The group that returned with the highest amount of coins used to win. At the end of the game, we had two things with us. First, a lesson that you must always take back what you've lost and second, a question that tested our character.

'Samarth,' called Aradhna Di. 'What will you do with the coins you've collected?'

Being the leader of my group, I came forward and opened my bag. I turned it upside down showing that it was completely empty.

'Oh! Why have you returned empty-handed?'

'Unfortunately, I could not find a single coin,' I said, closing the bag. 'But tomorrow if I win and fill up this bag, I would like to buy a good fortune for myself.'

Being a kid, I didn't know that you can never buy a good fortune. It'll favour you only when time is kind enough. When Prithvi presented his facts before us that day I felt that my bag was still empty. A good fortune was still out of sight.

'After those facts of Indian origin,' continued Prithvi, 'let me take your attention towards some facts related to human nature and behaviour. We humans behave differently in some situations. For instance, you may have noticed that when the batteries of your remote control wear out, you just push the buttons harder. Isn't that funny? The terminals of the battery don't get activated by pressing the buttons harder. *(Roar of laughter from the audience)*

And, these situations are created by none other than us ourselves, but we hardly give it a thought. Similarly, when you are using your computer and you notice a fly sitting on the monitor you tend to shoo it off by moving the mouse pointer around it instead of using your hands. *(Laughter continues)* Furthermore, when your alarm wakes you up early in the morning, you slam it irritatedly as it disturbs your sleep. But then, why do you again set the alarm at night? *(Laughter continues, supported by clapping)* All these are questions which only we humans can answer. With this, I end my speech and as I've promised, I took only 10 minutes from you, hoping that you enjoyed it. Thank you for your patient listening.'

As Prithvi ended, the silence in the audience broke and they gave a powerful round of applause to him, showing their satisfaction and approval. Their approval felt like a slap of defeat on our faces; we couldn't believe that after so much of hard work, we were most probably going to be defeated. Aarav sat down on one of the benches, holding his head, knowing it was all over. Tamanna was looking sadly towards the disappointed Aarav. I desperately turned towards the stage, unable to bear looking at the sad faces around me.

With that we end our competitive section and return to our other cultural programmes. Thank you very much to all our contestants.

Our next item is a band performance of our 11th standard students, ready to rock.

Within a few minutes of the announcement, the students came up on the stage with their guitars, drums, synthesizer, and other musical instruments. Theirs was the second last performance of the show and the next was ours.

'Come on students, we're next,' said Anjali Ma'am, preparing us. 'Follow me to the back of the stage.'

Everyone in the classroom got up and gathered their courage for the final show. Soon the classroom was empty, and we all piled up behind the stage. From there, we could see the large audience sitting in front of us. That view increased our anxiety levels. My legs were already trembling due to the extreme cold. It was 10:00 pm on my watch.

'Okay, my dear students, all the best for your performance,' said Ma'am, injecting a dose of motivation in all of us. 'Ours should be the best. One more thing—please don't panic or get flustered if you forget steps on stage, alright?'

Her way of talking had always been the plus point of her nature. She had a very generous way of talking to the students unlike the other teachers. We could hear the clapping noise from the audience indicating it was our turn on stage.

That was absolutely stunning. The next and the final performance for the night is a group dance from our 11th and 12th standard students; please welcome them with hearty applause!

'Finally, it's time,' I said to myself. The girls' group slowly came up on the stage. Our dance first started with them, while we boys entered a little later. With the lights scattered on all of them, Anjali Ma'am was ready to play the song, and we boys were ready supporting.

The music started to play. The girls began to dance under the starry night and the flickering lights. I was not feeling good seeing Aarav in such a sad state, he was showing no signs of enthusiasm or confidence. I prayed that he would dance well. There was just half an hour more for the end of this silver jubilee celebration and after that, we would be back home. I really wanted to be home. Suddenly, the music changed and now it was the boys' turn to enter onto the stage to dance along with the girls. I brought back my attention to the present and realized I needed to be focused on my dancing. Anjali Ma'am had planned a duet dance performance. I was dancing with Avni, Mihir with Sandhya, Youhaan with Suhaani, and Aarav with Tamanna. I don't know how coincidence played out so well that Ma'am had assigned the right partners for us. Aarav was dancing downheartedly. Tamanna had no option but to uplift his spirit and encourage him. Finally, our dance was finished. Thank God it went off well, unlike Aarav's competition which turned out to be an unexpected one.

That was a fabulous dancing performance from our senior students; they really took the stage and it was an awesome finale to our annual celebration.

'That was all I wanted, love you guys,' said Ma'am to all of us behind the stage while walking towards our classroom.

She was most happy with our performance and her joy could be seen in her eyes. Speaking personally, we were simply superb and definitely a treat for others' eyes. This performance really took the pain of Aarav's loss away from me.

Now I may please call upon our respected principal to come up on the stage and say a few words about this wonderful celebration which is now concluding.

Our principal stood up from his seat and started walking towards the stage. He must have definitely been feeling pleased that the function was a grand success. If, for me, it was far beyond my expectation, then for him it would have been a dream come true. With immense pleasure and pride, he came up on the stage and began to speak.

'It gives me a lot of happiness and joy to say that I have such a talented, versatile and capable bunch of students, creating a mesmerizing atmosphere over here. I would also like to thank my teachers for giving our students the right direction they needed. My special thanks to all the parents and guardians sitting in front of me who gave their valuable time just to attend the function, you all were a wonderful and inspiring audience for our students, as your applause is their motivation. My most grateful and special thanks to the God Almighty who has always blessed us. It gives me great honour now to present these trophies and certificates to my deserving students. May God bless you all, always.'

That was quite expected, we were not shocked, and I was ready to see Prithvi taking my brother's award. Even Aarav and others didn't seem to be very bothered about it.

First of all, I request the winners of the 'World's Amazing Facts' competition to come up and receive their awards. Starting with our third position, the award goes to Gyan Singh.

Gyan came up on the stage happily to receive his appreciation; the guy had given everyone good competition. Aarav was the runner up. Leaving all his regrets behind, Aarav started walking forward towards the stage to receive his award; there was a huge wave of clapping for him as he had indeed deserved it. It was a proud feeling for me to see him receiving an award.

Thank you, Aarav. Now comes our winner of the competition. He sealed his win when he appeared on the stage. Everyone put your hands together for Prithvi Mathur.

'Rubbish, I can't watch this,' said Mihir, seeing Prithvi receiving his award and the audience's attention.

Prithvi also received another award for being the school topper in the exams that had just concluded. After the stupid fellow went off the stage with his trophy, our principal again took hold of the mike to speak his final words.

'And that marks the end of this grand celebration, ladies and gentlemen. It's been a wonderful night, a memorable one for all of us. I have happy news for the students—from tomorrow, winter vacations will begin, lasting till 1st January. Are my students happy?'

There was huge noise from the students in all the classrooms and corridors shouting *yeeessss...* in unity, expressing their happiness. Within a few minutes, all the parents sitting in the audience stood up, the movement of chairs making plenty of noise. The audience that had been so calm now turned suddenly into a noisy crowd. They straightaway went to the respective classrooms to fetch their wards. The whole school was elated and intoxicated with the joy of winter vacations, except us four. We were gloomy and heartsick for two reasons—firstly, due to Aarav's loss and secondly, because we would not be able to meet the girls so freely for the coming few days. Pushing aside our gloomy thoughts, we picked our bags and went to search for our sisters. As we all reached the exit gate, we started wondering where our big sisters had gone, they were not visible anywhere.

'Are they too searching for us?' asked Avni.

We were clueless, both about our sister's whereabouts and the consequences that were in store for us. We had committed a blunder by dancing together. The harsh realization hit my head like a shooting arrow when one of my classmates came running towards us to deliver the bad news.

'I saw your sisters, they were sitting next to me,' said Gaurav, catching his breath. 'After your dance, I saw them getting up angrily and walking off in opposite directions. I think they didn't like your performance.'

Those words coming out of his mouth were like splashes of volcanic lava splashing onto our skins. We were so captivated by the charm of the function that we'd forgotten to follow the basic rule which had been imposed on us—to stay away from the girls. The serious repercussions of our forgetfulness were now waiting for us.

There's one more fact about good fortune that I must quote here. Once, I happen to read a book called *Puddn'head Wilson* in my school library. Though I'm not a voracious reader, it was an accidental read that I've always remembered. Written by one of the greatest writers of English literature, Mark Twain, the book talked about the hurtful beliefs of slavery and racism. The most significant learning I could take away from the story was a line that said, 'When ill luck begins, it does not come in sprinkles, but in showers.'

The Penalty Corner

Sunday mornings were always my favourite, getting up late and being lazy. I especially loved Sunday mornings in winter. But all the dreams of my winter vacation, of sleeping peacefully wrapped under the warm blanket, like an insect inside its pupa, were shattered. We four had to wake up early at 6:00 am and go jogging on the streets of Delhi when the other Delhiites were sleeping peacefully. This uphill task was given to us by our lovely Aastha Di as a punishment, because we danced with the girls. I still remember the conversation of that miserable night:

'So, all of you are back home,' asked Di in a ferocious tone. 'I thought you'd spend the night in the school campus.'

'Di, we were...we were,' said Youhaan, speaking hesitatingly. 'We were looking for you all around the campus.'

'Shut up, stupid,' I said to Youhaan under my breath.

'Okay, go to your room and sleep well,' said Di with a smile.

We couldn't understand then, the sarcasm in her smile when she said that. Where we thought she had simply forgiven us, she had already taken some big decisions. We all dashed into our room quickly as it was late, and we were already feeling drowsy. The night was extremely cold, so without wasting much time we just changed our clothes and jumped into our warm blankets.

'At last, feeling so good! Good night and sweet dreams,' said Mihir.

We slept as if the night itself was singing a soothing and harmonic lullaby for us. But the night got over too fast. It seemed as if we had fallen asleep just a few seconds ago. We woke up early at 6:00 am. Not intentionally, not by hearing any alarm, but yes, by Di herself. She just poured a full bucket of cold water onto our faces without any mercy. It felt as if the life force had left us when the icy water, like a thunderbolt, splashed onto our bodies. We leaped out of our beds, and standing in front was Di, holding the bucket in her hands.

'Hope you had a nice sleep, now it's time to work,' she said with the same smile that she displayed last night.

'What work?' asked Aarav.

We never realised that the work which she was talking about was this... jogging on the streets, battling the cold. Even the dogs on the street could snooze and it felt as if they were mocking us. A small mistake had brought upon us a heavy punishment that had ruined our vacations. That morning, the light was slowly coming up on the horizon, removing the remaining darkness over the atmosphere. Cold teeth-chattering winds were blowing over the land, which forced us to hold on to our jackets more tightly. There were dogs sleeping beneath parked vehicles and some under the minimal heat of street lights. We couldn't hear even the faint sound of any living species.

'Irritating cold, it's taking my life,' said Youhaan.

'Such a terrible punishment, totally unexpected,' I said.

'Aarav, why are you not saying anything? Are you loving this jogging?' asked Mihir.

'Nothing, let's get home quick,' said Aarav, deep in some thought.

It was 7:15 am when we were about to reach our building. By that time, the day had brightened. The sky was now a clear blue, awaiting the arrival of clouds; the sun still needed some time to establish its reign across the sky, while the cold winds continued blowing, with no mercy whatsoever. As we stopped in front of the entrance to our building to get some breath back and rest, a black shadow appeared in front of us. The shadow was none other than of Aradhna Di, who had a look of anger on her face.

'Listen, I am warning you all,' said Di, expressing her share of anger upon us. 'Stay away from my girls. That will be good for you.'

'But Di...' said Youhaan, not completing his sentence.

'I don't want any explanations,' said Di, cutting off Youhaan's words. 'You four morons can do whatever you want, but please don't include my girls in any of your activities.'

After warning us, she went off upstairs to her home. We four looked at each other, flabbergasted and thinking that nothing could be worse than this. If we were suffering with this harsh punishment given by Aastha Di who hated scolding us, then what would those girls be suffering, living with a person whose hobby was to punish?

'Hey Aarav, say something, you haven't spoken much since morning,' said Youhaan.

'I've nothing to say but I am sad,' said Aarav, with his face down. 'Not for being punished, but for what Aastha Di did. She didn't say a single word of appreciation for the award I got.'

He went upstairs slowly, carrying his disappointed face, and we four silently followed him. After having our bath, we promptly rushed to the terrace because we couldn't tolerate the cold anymore. Up there, the sun was smiling brightly on all the living species on earth. Our hands and feet which were chill and almost frozen, felt alive again. It slowly started to warm up. I felt as if the sun was erasing not only the cold but also my past memories which had darkened my heart. I was feeling relaxed when a funny scene grabbed my attention.

I saw all the four girls hanging washed clothes on the clotheslines. There were several buckets, all full of clothes.

'I think they washed all that stuff themselves,' I said.

'Oh God, that much?' said Youhaan.

The girls were not even looking towards us due to embarrassment. They rushed downstairs as soon as they finished their work.

'That's not a difficult punishment to accept, I imagined even worse,' said Aarav, lying down on the surface under the heat of the sun. He closed his eyes and went into some kind of quiet introspection.

'What are you doing?' asked Mihir.

Aarav didn't reply anything for a few seconds. After contemplating on something at length he spoke. 'I always wanted a quiet place to live my life,' he said. 'What if we had a world where reality was what we imagined?'

'I think you're hungry,' said Mihir and he was right. He said that on behalf of all of us. We started walking towards the stairs, talking about what could have been made for breakfast hoping it would be something delicious. When we entered, we could not see any food items placed on the table. We wondered what was happening.

'I think you all have a lot to study, isn't it?' said Di, suddenly coming from the kitchen.

'Yes Di, of course. We were just waiting for breakfast,' said Mihir.

'Breakfast? I am hearing this word for the first time, what does it mean?' asked Di.

We started wondering what Di was trying to say, her words had really left us confused. On the other hand, we were praying that what we were thinking should not come true.

'Breakfast is a simple word Di, it means breaking the fast of the night; you know we eat delicious dishes which make our day. It is often said that it is the most important meal of the day that helps us concentrate and build a strong metabolism,' said Mihir, swallowing some saliva into his gut. I saw Youhaan closing his eyes in disappointment, knowing what was about to come.

'Really, is it like that? I am so sorry, I didn't know anything about it. In other words, I haven't made anything for you,' said Di, her words hitting us like a heart attack.

'As expected,' I thought to myself.

After delivering her shocking news, she just walked away towards the kitchen to wash the plates kept in the sink, leaving Mihir in a state of mental shock with his mouth wide open.

'Are we in jail?' asked Aarav, as he passed by me to walk towards the bedroom.

We had no idea how to pass our time till lunch. Sitting in front of the books who were not our good friends, hearing the voices coming out from our empty stomachs, and looking outside the window was not at all enough for a good time pass. I saw Youhaan looking at the wall clock continuously, showing his impatience, Mihir making paper planes and flying it out of the window, Aarav staring at his trophy kept inside the shelf.

My mind was keen to find out what happened between Aastha and Aradhna Di that they had so much hatred in their hearts. Something awful must have happened between them. Maintaining a relationship riven with anger, they had always tried to keep the family ties intact. But sometimes, when ego ruled over common sense, they behaved belligerently.

However, after I managed to pass some time with my thoughts, I could feel the aroma of the afternoon preparations starting to waft in from the kitchen. It was a clear signal for us that we would definitely get our lunch. We knew that Di could not punish us for long; she loved us all very much. We passed our time inhaling those irresistible smells till we heard what we were patiently waiting for all this time.

'Lunch is ready, wash your hands and come to the table,' shouted Di.

Those golden words were like someone giving a free warm blanket to me to beat the cold. We all rushed towards the wash basin to wash our hands and with double speed we reached the lunch table where Di was already serving the food.

'One, two, and three,' I said, raising my fingers one by one. We rushed towards her and gave her a tight hug and said sorry.

'Let go of me and sit down,' said Di, still on a serious note. We quietly sat down on our chairs and started to stare at our plates. As soon as she completed her serving and sat down to eat, our hands were ready to just attack the delicious food. But my mind was preventing me from eating because I was not happy seeing her sad face. Somehow, I completed my lunch; my stomach was full, but my heart wasn't.

After a satisfying afternoon nap, I slowly opened my eyes. The evening had already arrived. I suddenly realized that we had to go to the temple at 7:00 pm; I kicked Mihir to wake him up and also the other two.

'What the hell?'

'Get ready fast, we have to go to the temple. I cannot handle any more punishments if we are late for any reason,' I said in a stubborn way.

The sound of the bells, the chanting of devotional songs and mantras, distribution of *prasad*, tying of sacred threads on the wrist, small children moving up and down the steps, were all a part of the temple atmosphere. I personally enjoyed it a lot. I loved to listen to the devotional songs played on the loudspeakers, they were an essential aspect of the temple environment. Whenever I entered the temple I felt as if I was not on earth but in a place where there was only divinity. While I was praying, Mihir suddenly came to me running.

'Where is Di?' asked Mihir.

'She must be here somewhere, but what happened?' I enquired.

'Aradhna Di is here. If they both meet, there's a possibility of a fight between them regarding the dance issue. So, be careful about them,' said Mihir in a frightened voice and he went off to complete his prayers. I started looking for Di but instead of her, I found Avni—she was looking breathtakingly beautiful. It took me some courage to stand in front of her and understand her state of mind.

'We are assigned to wash all the clothes including Di's until our vacations are over,' said Avni, expressing her irritation. We were standing in a corner and conversing, safe from the eyes of our sisters.

'Washing clothes, that's not a big deal.'

'Yes, but washing the clothes which are already washed and washing them twice a day is a big deal.'

I busted out laughing after hearing that.

'You think it's funny? No need to talk to me,' said Avni angrily and walked away.

'Wait, listen,' I shouted, but it was of no use. Avni was in no mood to listen.

While returning to our building, to our home, I was still thinking about what could be done to cheer up Avni. I needed to do something quickly because making up with her was a difficult task and she would not talk to me so easily. When my building was a little distance away, I looked towards the terrace of the girls' building and saw that a few clothes were still hanging on the ropes. Maybe the girls forgotten to take those. At that moment, an idea struck my deep, insane mind.

'You guys carry on, I am just coming in five minutes,' I said to the others.

'Where are you going?' asked Aarav.

'Nothing, I have some work. It'll not take much time,' I replied and I turned back, waiting for them to go. Soon they had gone upstairs and I reached the terrace of the opposite building to execute my plan.

Late at night, after having my dinner, I stood on the terrace of my building. I was waiting for Avni to come upon her terrace to collect the clothes. I wanted to cheer her up with the surprise I planned for her. Suddenly I saw the door of her terrace being opened. Out of all the moments which proved that hope never disappoints, this one was my favourite when Avni walked in. When she reached the ropes to take out the clothes, she was surprised to see what was hanging on the lines. Using the clothes hung there, I had made alphabets. I made an 'S,' an 'O,' 'R,' again an 'R,' and lastly, a 'Y.' Together they read 'SORRY.' Because of the darkness and the distance, I could not make that out clearly, but I was sure of the fact that she was smiling. I felt pleased then that she was no longer angry with me. That was enough for me to keep happily awake. I wished I could spend the night under the dark sky, beneath the light of the stars, and singing a song to beat the cold.

Love was something that I've always felt. I had never read about it in the legendary stories, nor had I heard about it from the greatest lovers in history. I could never understand why someone had to write about love in a larger than life way. Or why someone had to talk about it in a boastful manner. It almost forced me to believe that my understanding of love has always been weak. To clarify all my doubts, I summoned every ounce of courage and asked Di that night, 'Have you ever been in love?'

She couldn't answer it immediately as it was a question that had been rarely put to her in all these years. As a person who lived in a state of mind where responsibility had overpowered each and every emotion, she gathered some words to form an answer, which she thought was right.

'There's no direct answer to it,' she said. 'I might have but never bothered to realize it on time. Love has never been a necessity. It's not like money or food that I've to struggle for; instead, it's a simple thing.'

Her answer made me believe that love is perceived differently by different people. For some, it's an extraordinary feeling that transcends God, while for people like us, it's as common as a pack of bread. It doesn't matter how complex its definition becomes over time; the truth is, love is eternal.

The Proposal

'It's so good to sit here and watch the sky,' said Youhaan, while we were sitting on the roadside corner. If we turned back, we could clearly see the magnificent Red Fort.

'We've been sitting for a long time, I think we should move on,' I said.

'Correct. I can't handle this cold any more, let's get home,' said Youhaan, and he stood up forcefully, waking up Mihir who was still dozing peacefully. It was the second day of our jogging and we had to continue this routine for another nine days. We were sick of sacrificing our sleep for a silly mistake; at least those girls could sleep well, even though they had to wash clothes. The Red Fort was a few kilometres away from Chandni Chowk and from my point of view, we had come a long way. Slowly, the morning light crept into the sky and all around us. The streets were, as usual, empty at this time, and last but not the least, the cold breeze seemed to be taking our life. We were almost about to reach Chandni Chowk when suddenly, Youhaan shouted when he saw someone walking on the street.

'Hey look, who's that?'

'Relax, that guy is having his morning walk,' said Aarav.

'No guys, you are wrong,' I said, evoking a kind of curiosity among the three. 'He is someone familiar to me.'

'What do you mean?' asked Aarav.

'I can bet you that's Prithvi,' I said.

'Are you sure? And if you are sure, I've got a plan,' said Aarav, revealing his cruel intentions.

He convinced us with his inhumane, ruthless and uncivilized plan. We took out our handkerchiefs from our pockets and tied it across our faces to cover our identity. We started running towards Prithvi like bulls. We were like those wild bulls which run towards the matador with madness, but in this case the matador was clueless, and empty-handed without his *capote*. As soon as we approached him, Aarav gifted him with a strong kick of great force on his hips, as a result of which he collapsed on the ground. Then it was our role to perform, which we did quite efficiently. We started kicking him like a football, giving him no chance to escape whatsoever. He was like a frog, which by mistake, had come under the rolling wheels of a heavy moving vehicle. We kicked him repeatedly, showing no mercy at all. But suddenly, he stood up and gave a strong punch to Mihir's stomach, causing the latter to fall down and double up in excruciating pain. We were a little taken aback by this. He then caught hold of Aarav's throat so tightly that he started choking. I tried to remove his hands, but he held on firmly. He tried to remove Aarav's face cover but couldn't because Youhaan was hanging onto his back and blocking his hands. Suddenly, Mihir stood up and started shouting like a madman at Prithvi. Prithvi's strong kick landed on his stomach and gifted him a double dose of pain. Then, as his luck would have it, Mihir's handkerchief slipped and came off his face, falling to the ground.

'Mihir?' said Prithvi, breathing heavily. 'You are the SAMY's!'

Aarav' eyes were red, he was struggling to breathe and looked like he was almost on the verge of death. I decided it was time to stop this. I gave a strong push to Prithvi which caused him to let go of Aarav; after his hand been removed, Aarav started coughing badly. And yet, the anger within him pushed him to keep fighting. Finally, he was stopped, not by me but by someone else.

'Stop this nonsense! You'll hurt yourself very badly,' said Iqbal. He was the same man whom we had met that day while we were coming out of the café. And suddenly there was silence, complete silence; we all were looking at each other's hurt faces. Prithvi was bleeding from his mouth, Aarav was on his knees breathing heavily, Mihir was down holding his stomach, and I myself was standing with my hands on my hips, watching the man who was staring at us. My intuitions had come true and we had met him again.

'This is not right,' said Iqbal, scolding us. 'Fighting like street dogs at this age is not the mark of a disciplined human. I want everybody to say sorry to each other now.'

There was no response from anyone.

'Sorry is not a difficult word to pronounce.'

Slowly Prithvi approached Aarav and stopped right in front of him, staring aggressively into his eyes. I wondered what he was about to do.

'There will be a day,' said Prithvi, rubbing his bleeding lips. 'One day, when I'll give you a big shock. The shock will leave you completely bewildered,' he said and walked away from there. We all stood still, confused about what he actually meant. Maybe he was talking about taking his revenge.

'It seems that he is not one of your good buddies,' said Iqbal. 'Come, let's sit inside the park and relax.'

'No, thanks. We need to get home, it's already late,' I replied.

'You can at least spend 15 minutes with me whom you have met earlier also. Do you remember?'

'Yes, we remember you very well, but...' I said not completing my sentence.

'It's alright, come let's inhale some fresh air. You cannot go home in this manner, at least clean your clothes. Come.' His deep eyes were very persuasive. We couldn't say a firm 'no' and found ourselves saying 'yes' instead.

We entered the park along with him and sat under a tree on a wooden bench. We could hear the laughter of the senior citizens who were a part of the laughter club; many families were having a good walk and performing morning exercises in the background of the chirping birds. Human recreation and enjoyment were at its best. The park inside which we were sitting was the Mahatma Gandhi Park, located on the main Church Mission Road, near Chandni Chowk. We started to dust our clothes, clean our faces, and handkerchiefs and combed our hair down with our dirty hands.

'Boys, look at that nest on the tree top,' said Iqbal, sitting down on a bench. Attentively, we looked towards the tree as he continued, 'When the mother of those small baby birds goes out from her nest to fly in the immeasurable sky, she has a motive and an aim. Do you know what it is?'

'Yes, to get food for her hungry siblings,' answered Youhaan.

'Correct.'

'But what is the point? Why did you ask this question?' I enquired.

'It's simple. I want you all to learn something from that bird. Have some aim in your life, don't let it go wasted. According to me, every living species gets to live only one life. These myths of birth, re-birth and life-cycles are unknown to me. If I have a destiny to achieve, I have a life to live.'

No doubt, his words were inspiring, but what made me listen to him was when he said destiny. It again triggered my resentment towards life. His words struck like a revolutionary idea in my mind. I wondered how often it happens with me that I get affected by such profound thoughts. The last time it happened was while learning about great freedom fighters, like Chandrashekhar Azad, in the lessons of history. Incited by anger because of the Jallianwallah Bagh Massacre, Chandrashekhar Azad, along with other revolutionaries, dedicated his life to only one goal—freedom for the motherland. The British tried hard to capture and imprison him, but they failed every time because Azad was the master of disguises. Whether it was about teaching the local children of Jhansi under the name of Pandit Harishankar Brahmachari, blowing up the viceroy's train in the disguise of a sadhu, and disappearing in the crowd after avenging Lala Lajpat Rai's death, he evaded capture by the police on multiple occasions. It took the British Empire a reward of Rs. 30,000 to be announced on his head, finally leading them towards his whereabouts.

'Are you listening to me?' asked Iqbal after finding me lost in my own thoughts. I was not lost; I was briefly living that time of the Indian revolutionary movement. The part of Chandrashekhar Azad that profoundly inspired me was when he surprised death itself. When he was surrounded by police at the Alfred Park in Allahabad, injured and out of ammunition, he chose to shoot himself in the head instead of getting captured. He never failed his vow and thus set an irreplaceable mark of bravery. Through him, I realized that it is the bravery that always sets you apart from the ordinary.

'Are you with us?' asked Iqbal again.

'Of course,' I said, returning to the free nation where I breathed.

'You think we are aimless in life? Then you are wrong,' said Aarav in a flash.

'I'll be happy if proved wrong,' said Iqbal confidently. With his experience, he could easily determine our situation.

'When I was a child, I discovered that I was born to serve my country. I don't know when this feeling of patriotism emerged within me which naturally told me to join the army. And today, I am happy in the service of my country, and sacrificing my sleep so that my fellow countrymen can sleep peacefully.'

'We also have patriotic feelings inside us,' said Mihir. 'We ensure our attendance in school during every Independence Day and Republic Day celebrations.'

Iqbal laughed at his innocent answer and said, 'so, you call that patriotism? That much, every citizen can do for his country. You must do something big to be recognised in your own nation.'

'And how can we achieve that?' I asked.

'Are you serious in asking this question?'

'Yes, I am very serious. I am tired of this sick way of living and I want to have my own identity. These humiliations, restrictions, and instructions which I get create some sort of madness in me. Today, I know the world and tomorrow I want the world to know me. Today if I celebrate my birthday, I want the world to celebrate it along with me,' I said.

Iqbal was silent for a moment and then he asked, 'Is this the condition with everybody?'

We all nodded our head, giving the answer to his question. He thought again for a moment by closing his eyes and folding his hands. We were very curious to know his answer.

'I think you are destined to do this,' said Iqbal and he stood up. He walked towards us and said a few words which I could never forget. 'I am looking for some young people,' he said, 'who are brave enough to do this job, and seeing the ignited spirit inside you, I think you all seem to be perfect.'

'What job?' I asked.

'We are a small army group of 9-10 jawans who are living here in Delhi-6 for a short period of time. We are here for some investigative work, based on the probability of a terrorist attack according to our intelligence reports.'

We were stunned to hear that. There was a threat to the city where we lived and to our nation. While we were still absorbing the intensity of this news, he continued.

'Till the time we are here, we cannot afford to reveal our identity to others. We need to live like the common inhabitants here. I need to make sure that the people living here should not have to experience a panic situation in their daily lives.'

'What are we supposed to do?' I asked.

'The point is, we need a place to hide our weapons and ammunition till we complete our investigative work. The area and the house in which we are living is not a safe place to keep our arms. This place is still not familiar to us, so we need the help of local inhabitants. You seem to be the perfect ones to handle this.'

We looked at each other's faces after hearing those words. The challenge was quite a difficult one, but we were in no mood to stay away from it.

'If we tell you the places, can't you do this job on your own?' asked Aarav.

'No, because we need to concentrate on our investigative work more. Any misunderstanding in that work can be a blunder. Think twice before giving an answer.'

We were still thinking with our heads down. It was a difficult job to perform and a difficult decision to make. A 'yes' could change our lives forever while a 'no' would lead us back to our old life. I took a deep breath, closed my eyes and recollected the events of the past few days. Every instance of my past life, whether good or bad was rolling like a film reel in my mind and I said to myself , 'Every moment is already written and destined, including this one.'

'Take as much time as you want to think,' said Iqbal. 'There's no hurry.'

'Give us a date and place,' said Aarav. 'We'll be present there with a final decision.'

After hearing our answer, he stood up taking a heavy breath, looked towards the sky and started speaking.

'Remember one thing, if you agree to do this, then our work should remain confidential, not a single word is to be uttered to your friends, family members, and neighbours. Is it crystal clear?'

'Consider it a promise,' said Aarav.

'Well and good. Meet me on the day of Christmas. Meet me here this same place at 8:00 pm, with your decision,' said Iqbal and he went away from there, leaving us alone. We watched him till he was out of the park gate; we all looked at each other and smiled as a sign of satisfaction that what we had done was right. It was 8:00 am on my watch and I realized that it was too late to get home.

When we reached our building, we saw Desai Uncle getting out from an auto. Desai Uncle was finally home after a few days of medical treatment. Everyone was happy to see him back but there was one who was very happy to see him.

'Uncle, you are back,' shouted Mihir happily.

'Yes son, by God's grace,' replied Desai Uncle.

'Doctor has advised him to take rest,' said Aunty, showing her concern.

'Let's get inside,' said Desai Uncle.

'Uncle, wait, I want to tell you something,' said Mihir stopping them.

'What?'

'I promise you that I'll never disturb you anymore. You will face no more tension because of me,' said Mihir with a cute smile. Then, suddenly he started vomiting on the mud-guard of his scooter, out of tiredness. He must have been felt exhausted after that long-distance jogging and the fight that followed.

'Please take me inside before it's too late for me,' said Uncle, almost in tears.

'Mihir, are you alright?' asked Di, quickly reaching him. She took him slowly upstairs.

'Some things never change,' I said to myself as I followed Di and my brothers.

But change has always been a factor, even in the process of human evolution. Changes do happen, sometimes drastically. The day we met Iqbal marked the first change in our tumultuous daily life. At last, we would've something where the investment of time was worth it. Or, it seemed to be. Mihir had a new companion, a foe turned friend who now didn't mind sitting and talking with him.

'Uncle, tell me something,' said Mihir, sitting beside Desai uncle in his home. 'Did the Arab ever meet that thief again?'

'I don't think that could've ever happened,' said Desai uncle, tossing a tablet into his mouth and swallowing it with a glassful of water. 'Why would you meet someone who was supposed to do something wrong?'

'But he didn't do it.'

'We're not taking sides here, are we?' asked Desai uncle, looking at Mihir puzzlingly. 'Listen, not all those who have chosen the wrong way of living will backout one day. That thief did, but he might be one out of a thousand.'

Desai uncle's thoughts, out of his personal experience, didn't meet Mihir's expectations. Mihir was confused about what made that thief one out of a thousand. Before he could solve it, there was more to add up to it.

'The thief has to prove his nature,' said Desai uncle. 'He has to re-establish the belief in the people to whom he had caused severe losses. Then, maybe one day, the Arab will consider meeting him.'

It would take another Christmas for Mihir to derive the meaning of those words, but until then, he could keep it as a valuable present. He looked at the clock and realized it was about time that he returns home and take rest. A new day was waiting for all of us.

Merry Christmas

There was just one day to go for Christmas. In Delhi, Christmas is a time for shopping, relaxing and partying. This year too, the whole of Delhi was caught up in Christmas fever. Homes and streets are decorated beautifully with lights and coloured stars. The city turns red and green with the Christmas spirit. The celebrations are, of course, incomplete without Santa Claus. Days before the actual festival, Santa Clauses can be seen roaming around and distributing gifts at a number of places. All my life, I have known only two Santa Clauses. During my orphanage days, Aastha and Aradhna Di used to wear the white fur-trimmed red suit and stocking cap with a sack full of gifts on their back. They distributed gifts to all the children in the orphanage. For me, the biggest gift that they gave me was my life itself. I could've never wasted it. All these years, though I've not been able to do something good, I've never made her regret that giving me life was a mistake.

'Samarth come down quickly, we've something to show you!' I heard someone calling me when I was thinking about all this. I looked down the window and saw Mihir and Youhaan waving their hands, signalling me to come downstairs. I wondered what was so exciting that they were not able to control it; I reached for my jacket as it was 5:00 pm and the cold wind was really strong. When I reached downstairs, they both just held my hand and started running by pulling me.

'Guys, I think you are not satisfied with our jogging in the morning, isn't it?' I asked.

'Just shut up and come with us, there is a surprise on the way,' said Youhaan.

We ran a long way and finally stopped alongside the west gate of Jama Masjid, lying at one end of a very busy central street of Old Delhi, the Chawri Bazar Road. Built in red sandstone and marble by more than 5000 artisans, this outstanding architectural masterpiece projects beautifully into the Old Delhi skyline. At the bottom of the Masjid stairs, I saw a girl sitting. She looked as if she was desperately waiting for someone.

'That's Tamanna right?' I enquired.

'Yes,' replied Youhaan. 'We brought you here because we think that Tamanna came here to declare her love.'

I was not able to believe what Youhaan said, I was absolutely dumbstruck and speechless.

'Just look at his face, Youhaan,' said Mihir, pointing to me and laughing.

'But how did you both find out?'

'You forget brother, I am a Sherlock Holmes fan, it was too easy for me,' said Mihir.

'But how did you, Mihir?'

'Today, I saw a letter from Tamanna in Aarav's school bag; it contained the address of the meeting place. Maybe she put this letter into his bag secretly before the holidays.'

'But Sherlock Holmes got very difficult cases.'

'Ssshhh,' said Youhaan, keeping his finger on his lips. 'Aarav is coming.'

We saw Aarav walking towards her, slowly emerging from the crowd. Tamanna saw him and got up, displaying her beautiful smile, the smile which she always broadcast upon seeing Aarav. When love happens, the wonders around you become ineffable. Strangers seem to be your best friends, the heart seems to be beating at 90 beats per minute and during nights, instead of sleeping, you watch the image of moon sailing on the surface of water. Like every other ordinary girl, Tamanna was undergoing the same emotions. In no time, I was sure that a nice, romantic scene was on the way. I was very happy for Tamanna that she had finally decided to convey her feelings for him. Very soon, before me were standing Aarav and Tamanna, looking into each other's eyes affectionately in the background of the setting sunlight with the beautiful pigeons flying over the dome of the mosque.

'Can we go for a walk?' asked Tamanna and Aarav agreed immediately. They started walking for a few minutes without saying anything to each other. They finally stopped after walking a considerable distance and then stood still. We reached a convenient position from where we could hear their voices quite clearly without their becoming aware of our presence. I could clearly feel her happiness. The way she was staring at Aarav, it seemed that she was already dreaming of a successful relationship. Like in an unreal and larger than life romance, she was already visualising Aarav and herself in the cold, snow-filled valleys of Kashmir, her favourite place. Perhaps she imagined herself standing on one of the snow-laden lanes of Gulmarg while Aarav approached her slowly, singing, then moving his fingers down her cheek and she blushing away cutely. Perhaps she imagined him singing for her while they stood amidst the beautiful tulips of the Mughal Gardens, comparing her beauty to the tulips. Did she delight in the dream of them both playing together in the vast and open area of the Gulmarg golf course? Or thrill to the thought of him splashing a few drops of water from the Dal Lake on her face to see her reaction?

'You want to say something to me?' asked Aarav, suddenly bringing her into reality where she was surrounded by the horns of the moving vehicles and daily commotions of life.

'Yes, I am just wondering from where I should start,' said Tamanna, feeling a little hesitant. 'We have known each other for a very long time,' she continued, 'and from the time we came to know each other, something is running in my heart constantly, but I am unable to share it.'

Aarav knew what she was about to say but still allowed her to complete herself.

'When I see my sisters in happy relationships,' said Tamanna, 'I feel upset wondering why there is a distance only between the two of us. I want to erase this distance forever. I was short of courage in doing that. I only wished I could have done it little earlier.'

'Please don't mind when I say this but you're confusing me,' said Aarav.

'Is he mad?' asked Mihir angrily.

'Keep quiet idiot, listen to what they are saying,' I said and turned my focus back on Aarav and Tamanna.

'You are pretending as if you don't know anything,' said Tamanna disappointingly. 'You know that I love you from the bottom of my heart. This attitude of yours is hurting me because I know even you love me.'

'I don't think so,' said Aarav.

'You don't know how to express it, but I know. Listen Aarav, your presence always gives me happiness and I can't even measure my love when you are around me. The only thing missing in my life is you and I want to complete that space.'

'It's just not possible, I never thought about you in that way.'

'Then why did you come here when I called you?'

'Just to say you should stop hurting yourself. We cannot have a happy relationship when there are so many restrictions around us. Moreover, I don't deserve your love. I came here to tell you to love that person who deserves your love.'

'You are that deserving person. In this life and our future lives, it's only you. My soul rests inside you. I love you so much.'

A tear rolled down Tamanna's cheek.

'I am sorry, I can't do this,' said Aarav, and he slowly retreated. But seeing Tamanna crying, he turned back for a moment and stopped. 'I wish we belonged to an ideal world,' he said and resumed walking.

'Why does he keep saying that?' I thought as I watched Tamanna crying in despair. Aarav just left her in the middle of the crowd, ignoring her emotions. When the heart breaks, it feels like someone has stopped the hands of the clock, it feels as if you are the last human on earth.

Tamanna's dreams of the beautiful Kashmir Valley had been transformed harshly into a cyclone of nightmares. It was very difficult for her to forget the face that she had loved since she was a child. For her, Christmas will never be the same.

The arrival of Christmas marked some twists in our family. The four of us had to meet a man, whom we didn't knew at all. His arrival into our lives was very strange and I still didn't know why we felt weak in front of that strangeness. Aastha Di, who was angry, was slowly turning back into that old cheerful being. But the most hurtful twist was about Tamanna. The previous evening had changed her life. I saw her sitting at her bedroom window sadly, looking outside and remembering her heart-breaking evening. She was like a dried, hardened leaf that would crumble if you stepped on it.

'Are you dreaming, brother?' asked Youhaan, placing his hand on my shoulder.

'Not at all,' I said, as I turned back towards him.

'Here, eat this tasty, yummy, super delicious plum cake,' said Youhaan.

'Great, who brought this?' I enquired.

'Me,' said Aarav.

'I am not in a mood, thank you,' I said ignoring him.

'You three have been behaving differently since night,' said Aarav, frustrated.

We were angry with Aarav after what he did yesterday and were ignoring him as much as possible. For what he did, he deserved a bigger punishment.

'Guys, let's get serious now,' said Youhaan. 'Today at 8:00 pm, we've to meet Iqbal and tell our decision. Have you thought about that?'

'Don't worry, there's still plenty of time left,' I said in a comforting way and started walking out of the room.

The night arrived with infinite bundles of darkness and sparkling stars. It was like a black blanket designed with shining stars, covering the whole of Delhi from the icy cold, but to no avail. Winter's grip on the city had grown too powerful. I was alone standing on the terrace of my building. I could see the bustling streets which are never quiet. One can talk about the hot, tasty delights being fried at different corners, eateries which have won the hearts of millions of Indians and people from different countries, shops set up in the narrow lanes offering a variety of things. I felt proud to stand on the terrace of one of the buildings in Chandni Chowk, a space whose roots go deep into the history of India.

'It's 7:30 pm,' someone shouted from behind, disturbing the solitude that prevailed around me.

'What?' I asked as I came back to the terrace from the streets, and when I turned, it was Aarav whom I saw.

'You are dreaming today, what happened?' asked Aarav.

'No, I think you have a misconception.'

'Really? Do you know what day is today?'

'Of course, Christmas for sure.'

'And?'

'And what?'

'Just half an hour is remaining for our meeting; don't you think we are late already?' asked Aarav. 'I told you, come back to reality.'

'We are late,' I said, looking at watch. I was about to run downstairs when Aarav stopped me and asked, 'We're doing this, right?'

I couldn't reply to him honestly that time and I just nodded my head. Soon we reached down to the streets and into the crowd; I looked up towards the window of my room where Di was sitting and experienced some unusual feelings. I felt as if I was creating a huge distance between me and Di; at the same time, I felt as if some invisible force was trying to prevent me from going ahead.

'Come on Samarth, we are getting late,' shouted Youhaan, and I started running again towards the new fate that was awaiting me and my brothers.

We reached the park five minutes late. We looked around for Iqbal but he was nowhere to be seen. We were roaming in the park all by ourselves, bounded by the green trees. The calmness all around was a soothing relief from the tensions and worries of my daily life.

'Sorry, I am late,' said a voice suddenly, and when we looked back, it was the man whom we were searching for. He had one white bag slung across on his shoulders and two in his hands.

'It's okay, actually we too arrived late,' said Mihir.

'I am not very free even on Christmas Day. We need to hurry, there's lot of work to be done. And Happy Christmas, by the way,' he said in a serious tone.

'Same to you,' said Mihir.

'Okay, without wasting time, let's come to the point,' said Aarav.

'Yes, so what have you decided?'

We four started to stare each other, our faces and minds were totally blank as we had no answer.

'Be quick, I don't have much time.'

'We're ready for it,' I said. 'On behalf of my three brothers and myself, our answer to your offer is a 'yes'

'Are you sure?' confirmed Iqbal.

'Our decision is final, there's no looking back from here on,' said Aarav.

'I kind of anticipated your answer,' said Iqbal, putting down all the bags. 'Tell me the place where you are going to keep this.'

We all thought hard for a moment. Everything was happening so quick that we were afraid if we have set out on the right path. We had agreed to achieve something without knowing the way. Not wasting any more time, I said the name of the first place that randomly came to my mind.

'Our school,' I said.

'*Whaaaat?*' shouted my three brothers in shock. They glared at me. Mihir caught hold of my shoulders and started shaking me, saying, 'Are you mad?'

They all started shouting at me in anger. 'Wait, hold on, let him speak,' shouted Iqbal.

'We know each and every corner of our school,' I started explaining, 'from the main gate to the different corridors. I know some secret places which even our principal is unaware of. It's vacation time and there will be no one present in the school compounds, it's the best time to start with the job,' I said.

I looked towards my brothers after completing my sentence, but they were in a state of dismal shock. When I looked towards Iqbal, he was thinking of something very deeply, his seriousness clearly reflected in his eyes.

'Why does this guy always think so much?' I thought to myself.

After thinking for a while, he put his hands into the pocket of his trouser and took out a fresh bundle of Indian currency notes.

'Offer accepted, here is your first reward.'

The four of us gaped, mouths wide open at that bundle of money. We had never seen so much money like that.

'Rs. 10,000, use it wisely.'

'We cannot take this, it's so much money,' said Aarav.

'For what all of you are doing, you deserve much more. Don't hesitate, it belongs to you.'

We tried our best to refuse his offer, but his persuasive words finally obliged us to accept it. Money is a dangerous commodity. It becomes even more dangerous when associated with certain inflammable things. The global recession of 2009 taught me that if money is insufficient to meet your requirements, it can devastate the world. This stagnation in economic growth caused millions of people to lose their jobs and homes. Though less severe than a global economic decline, if money is insufficient to meet your greed and need, it can still have significant consequences. Aastha Di once told us about an accountant working in her office who was terminated after being accused of theft. He stole money that resulted in a big loss of revenue. The third time when I learned the power of money was when Iqbal handed over the bundle of currency notes to us. What would've been the result when money was associated with fame, I thought.

'Good, take these bags. They contain important things; you have to secure them. Goodbye!' said Iqbal and he started walking towards the exit gate, leaving us with the money and bags in our hand. We were silent for a few minutes, thinking and wondering. Was it a dream?

'Happy Christmas everyone, enjoy the night, let's have a party!' shouted Mihir as he started jumping with excitement. There were smiles on our faces. Our Christmas night became merrier, the cloud of strangeness that had surrounded me suddenly vanished, and the cold winds that were blowing appeared to be friendly.

I once again looked at the money I held in my hands. It is often said that staying still and calm after a snake bite prevents the venom from spreading faster in the body. Money was the same poison for me. I had to use it wisely and intelligently to avoid the poisonous greed to infiltrate my mind.

Living a Secret Life

The entire night we talked about heroes—caped crime fighters, vigilantes, and masked heroes. Some were chosen by nature while some by the act of their will. They all lived a life for the betterment of others. Not worrying a single day about their own identity, they relentlessly fought against the wrongdoers.

'So, does our future look bright now?' asked Mihir, standing on the terrace with me, while Aarav and Youhaan had already slept.

'We never know what the future is,' I said, breathing the air of unknown possibilities. I could've romanticized about my unforeseen future, but I chose not to. My mind was stuck in a dilemma—were we the chosen ones, or was it our disposition towards recognition that made us take that decision? The riddle was as strong as the mystery of destiny for me.

Destiny, again and again, reminded me that my failure to understand it was the biggest flaw of my life. This discomfiture still bothered me when I stood at the gate of my school the next night.

'Samarth,' called Aarav, shaking me. 'How do we enter inside?'

We all reached our school in different rickshaws with bags on our shoulders. It was easy for us to find a way to reach here but not to enter inside.

'Let's get in through the back wall,' I said. 'First I'll jump and you two follow me.'

I climbed the back wall and jumped into the school premises with the heavy load of the bag on my shoulders. It boggled my imagination that one day I would be entering my school like a thief.

'I am in,' I said. The others followed. The three of us started walking patiently without making any kind of noise. I was leading the way, with Youhaan in between and Aarav bringing up the rear end. Our eyes darted here and there to check for anyone spying on us. At some distance, we saw the guard sitting on the chair and enjoying his cigarette.

'How will we cross him?' asked Youhaan.

'I have a plan to distract him,' said Aarav.

He took a stone lying nearby and threw it with full force. The stone hit the garden making a dull sound in the bushes. The guard got alert and went to check the garden side. We got our much-awaited chance and crossed him without coming under his notice.

Back at home, we had put on our thinking cap and had already decided a place to hide the bags. Our chemistry lab. I opened the lock of the lab with the help of a hair clip that I had brought from my home. Yes, disregarding all technologies, we still had locks that could've been opened with just a hair clip. While I was opening the lock, my brothers kept guard against any likely spies. We finally entered the lab, carrying the bag on our shoulders.

The chemistry lab has always been a weird place for me. The place was full of complex chemicals, strange experiments, and the unintended results that I derived from them.

'Samarth,' called my chemistry teacher. 'Can you write the chemical equation when hydrochloric acid reacts with zinc metal?' Suddenly I was back to a past moment of my life where my chemistry teacher was demonstrating an experiment to study the properties of acids and bases. It was the day when I realized that the chemistry between humans was not less complicated than the chemistry between chemical substances.

I went towards the blackboard and stood there like a silly ass. As expected, I ended up writing the wrong equation.

'Do you even know what we're doing right now?' asked my teacher sarcastically, questioning the blankness on my face. 'Aarav, could you please go and correct him?'

Aarav, as dumb as me, started correcting my wrong equation. He would've made more errors if Tamanna was not there to save him. I saw her giving silent indications to him, trying to tell that he should write the number 2 in front of hydrochloric acid and as a subscript with chlorine in zinc chloride.

Aarav at last corrected my unbalanced equation, saving himself from another embarrassment. The rule says that to form a balanced equation, the number of atoms of each element of reactants should be equal to the number of atoms of each element of products. Where I missed this basic rule, Aarav perfectly captured it, both in the class and in his life. He, who always ignored Tamanna, chose to take her help to save his pride. Did he take love for granted? I could never understand that situation, nor did I understand this one where I was standing inside the same lab, but empty.

'Where shall we keep this?' asked Aarav, bringing me back to the present.

'Please tell us quickly, this stuff is too heavy,' said Youhaan.

Inside the lab there was a small place just below the roof, a kind of loft space to keep things and unused items. Rarely had I seen anyone getting up there and picking up any items. For me, it was a safe place to start with.

'We will keep it there,' I said pointing my finger towards the loft.

'There? Are you sure?' asked Aarav.

'You've any other place in your mind?' I asked.

'No,' he replied.

We took a stool from the lab; it was not an ordinary stool but was a tall one. Our lab assistant would use it whenever he wanted to take any chemicals or salts from the other shelves that were used. I stood up on the stool; my height was quite enough so that I could reach the place easily. It was very dark inside, making it difficult for me to look around properly.

'Give me the torch,' I said, and Youhaan handed over a torch to me.

Switching on the torch and holding it with my mouth, I jumped into the store with the bag on my shoulder. I took the other two bags from my brothers and pushed them all deep inside the place. I covered them with other stuff so that no one could see them. But then, I began to sneeze really hard, thanks to my dust allergy.

'Get down,' shouted Youhaan in a low voice as we heard the sound of the whistle outside. The guard got alerted due to my uncontrollable sneezing. My nose started to curl up and I was about to sneeze one more time when Mihir covered my mouth tightly.

'Shut up you fool,' he said, covering my mouth. But the pressure of expulsion was too much to handle for me and I ended up spitting saliva on his palm.

'Yuck,' reacted Mihir, wiping his hands on his shirt. Youhaan was quick enough to pull all of us to a corner when he heard the sound of muffled footsteps outside. As the sounds grew heavier as they came nearer, our heart was in our mouth.

'If he finds the lock opened, he'll surely get in,' said Aarav. We saw the light from the guard's torch being illuminated on to the windowpanes. It was a clear indication that the guard was very near.

'Look for things that are hard,' I said, setting up everyone to a quick task. They all started searching and returned with long beakers, boiling & volumetric flasks, and graduated cylinders.

'We're not going to kill him, right?' asked Mihir, holding the volumetric flask tightly by its long neck and standing in an attacking position.

'No,' I said, dismissing his doubts. 'We're just going to put him into a small nap.'

We all stood at the door, holding our apparatus and ready to hit the guard when he opens the door. It was a terrible choice but also the last option. We could feel his presence right outside the door, and it was just a matter of time until we're exposed. Either we hit him or avowedly register our names on the list of terminated students from the school.

The guard saw the lock of the lab opened. He started examining it to find out how it was left open while the four of us were already sweating inside. Just when he was about to open the door, his attention got diverted towards a distant sound. The guard was not sure what it was, maybe a cat jumping on the benches, rattling sound of a loosely closed window, or a dull thud coming from two classrooms away. Whatever be the source of that sound, for us, it was an intervention of divine power. We heard the sound of the footsteps going in the other direction and gradually fading. After a few minutes, we were sure that it was safe to get out.

'He's gone, let's get out of here,' I said, keeping the beaker back at its place.

We opened the door, checked the surroundings to ensure it was absolutely clear and started running towards the back wall from where we climbed in. As we were running, we suddenly saw a figure in front of us, and we were startled. Luckily, he was not facing us, instead, he was admiring the starless night sky. We quickly hid to a corner near the staircase that led to the junior section.

'A second guard?' said Mihir, breathing fast. 'When did our school hire a second guard?'

We had no answer to that question. All we could do is to peek and see what he was doing. He seemed less active and vigilant as compared to the other guard who was in service for a long time. He was only crooning some old Hindi songs and was enjoying the cool breeze.

'Come on, start moving,' said Aarav, looking at the guard who was the only obstacle between us and the exit point. He watched the guard without a blink until he stopped singing and turned towards him surprisingly.

'Shit!' exclaimed Aarav meekly and turning away. 'I think he saw me.'

'Idiot,' said Mihir, expressing his annoyance. 'Is there anything that you can do properly?'

'Hush! Keep quiet all of you,' I shouted as unobtrusively as possible. The guard let out a whistle and started walking towards the place where we were hiding. I could hear the clacking sound of his stick as it hit the concrete floor. Mihir stood beside me, tightly clutching my hands in nervousness while I thought our assignment was about to complete before it started.

Dada...called the guard, addressing the other guard as his elder brother to check whether it was him. Hearing no response, he continued walking, lighting his torch.

Batsal...we heard a shout from the corridor. It was the other guard who was calling out his colleague. From his alarming voice, it was clear that suspiciousness had got hold of him. His sixth sense had warned him that someone had entered the school.

Batsal...check the corridor. The guard shouted again.

Hearing his name being called by his senior twice, the newcomer dismissed his vision as just another mild hallucination and ran towards the corridor. More than his sensory perceptions, he believed in a man who spoke from experience. As he went past us blowing whistles, we prayed that he doesn't turn back and end our miserable adventure.

'Remove your shoes,' I said softly. 'Run and don't turn back.'

Obeying my words, the three of them held their shoes in hands and prepared themselves to run. We finally got a clear window and ran towards the wall as fast as possible. At last, we jumped out, safe and sound. We started giggling nervously, thinking about what happened inside a few moments ago. We were successful in completing what was assigned to us. That success intoxicated us, making us unaware of the fact that we had changed something. We had let inside a strange force that till now used to roam around the boundaries of the city. That unknown force was now slowly beginning to dominate the atmosphere in which we breathed.

'Let's move,' I said, heedless of the sparks that could lit and kindle violent fire.

A Great Escape

Five days passed after the Christmas festival got over and the whole world was on the verge of starting another new year. We too were taking full rest in our home after completing our first assigned job and yes, there was no more jogging in the morning as our angry sister had gone back to being her sweet and lovely self. As for the cold, it was getting more and more intense as each hour passed.

'I am waiting for the school to reopen,' said Aarav, as we watched a Hollywood movie.

'Why are you so eager? Change the channel please,' said Mihir.

'Take it and keep it with you,' said Aarav, throwing the remote angrily towards him.

'Control yourself, dude,' said Mihir.

'Easy, guys,' I said, calming them both.

We were still irritated with Aarav for what he had done on Christmas Eve. The image of Tamanna's crying face was still in my mind; it was the reason I couldn't easily forgive Aarav.

'You guys have changed so much,' said Aarav while Mihir changed the channel.

'Who doesn't like a change?' said Youhaan.

We were not giving him the answers he wanted to hear and that was our way of irritating him. While Aarav was about to speak, we saw something on the television screen that was terrifying. It stopped all of us from speaking. My heart was pounding and the four of us were just glued to the TV screen. The news anchor said:

A low intensity bomb explosion took place in this part of Chandni Chowk two hours ago injuring a few people who have been rushed to the hospital immediately.

Aastha Di rushed in from the kitchen and she was horrified seeing the images shown in the news.

The explosion took place in that tea shop which you can see behind me. The tea shop has been badly damaged, and the bomb squad is still working to find the root cause.

The images of the burned tea shop from all different angles, people injured, blurred images of a few dead bodies, all were continuously being displayed on the TV screen. The images were haunting and horrendous. I stood up and started walking towards the terrace to get some fresh air as I could not bear it any longer. When I reached the terrace, the sunlight was about to arrive, a clear blue sky was floating above me, and a cold wind was whispering in my ears. I turned my head and looked towards the plants in their pots; they were in a bad state, all dried up and the soil was also somewhat dry, waterless.

'Aarav is so irresponsible,' I said to myself.

I went downstairs and brought up a bucketful of water and a mug. I took a full mug of water and started watering the plants, starting from the soil to their leaves. I wanted a way to pass the time and forget those horrible images that I saw on TV. I wanted to engage myself in some work or other which would help me in doing this.

'What are you doing here?' asked Di, entering the terrace suddenly.

'Nothing, they all are dried up,' I said in reply.

She slowly came towards me took the mug away from my hand, hugged me, and said, 'Don't worry, I know you are afraid. Just relax, I am there with you.'

At that moment, I thought of admitting everything about what we had been doing during the past five days, but something stopped me from going ahead again. The perpetrated acts of terrorism were spreading like a plague in the country. Everyone was terrified. I had no words to express my grief. All I could do was to believe in the path chosen by me to defeat terrorism.

The bomb blast had become the hot topic of conversation for the people that day. There were discussions going on in the houses, on the streets and even at the eatery shops where we were enjoying tasty *dahi bhallas*. There were only a few eatery shops that were open on that evening. Many people stayed indoors which was why Chandni Chowk was less crowded that day. Di allowed us to come out after many requests, appeals, begging, and pleading. She gave us a time limit at last and regulated us to remain within the time limit. There were many discussions taking place around me while I was having my delicious snack.

I think it's becoming impossible to uproot terrorism from this country.

Absolutely, even now when I am standing here, I am scared.

Our ancestors told us that God has decided a specific time for all of us to die, but now it has changed. Death is following us every minute.

It is not just one country that can completely eradicate the roots of terrorism. The world has to be united against it and develop effective counterterrorism to end it ultimately.

'We should go,' said Youhaan after hearing all those remarks.

We started moving from there when someone caught hold of my shoulder and forced me to stop. I turned back. 'We need to talk,' said Iqbal who was standing behind me.

'Do you know what happened?' I asked, almost furiously.

'Yes, I do,' he said, adjusting his winter cap so that it covered his ears.

'Then why don't you do anything? Go and find out who is responsible for this,' said Mihir.

'It's not that easy,' he said, putting his hand on my shoulders. He started walking along with us and continued talking. 'The blast was totally unexpected. We had no idea that something like this was going to happen.'

He sounded right at that moment. Sometimes even with the highest degree of intelligence available to you, a failure cannot be avoided. 'You four don't get tensed about the bomb blast,' he said, 'it's our duty to bring the culprit into the hands of the law. For you all, there's a job waiting to be done tomorrow.'

'And what is it?' asked Aarav.

'You have to reach the railway station. There are two bags which have to be kept in your school.'

'Are you sure?' enquired Youhaan, feeling doubtful. 'There's a lot of security in the railway station. Who will hand it over to us there?'

'Everything will be taken care of,' assured Iqbal. 'You reach there by 10:00 am and the bags will be handed over to you.' He went away after saying that, repeating his usual habit. Sometimes I felt that the man was like smoke. He simply dissipated into the air.

At the station, we were confused as to how this all was going to happen. We were in the midst of deafening whistles, lightning fast trains, goods and carriages, loads of luggage, lakhs of passengers, and plenty of emotions. In middle of the restaurant facilities, departures and arrivals boards, luggage carts and waiting rooms, we were madly searching for the man who would hand us the two bags, but the problem was that we didn't know his face. We were roaming on one of the platforms of the second busiest and one of the largest stations in India.

I was slowly getting irritated as we were totally wasting our time standing and watching the trains passing by. Furthermore, we had come there without informing Di, knowing she would kill us if she came to know about our escapade.

'You told Di that we are going to buy some books and believe me, it was a good excuse,' said Mihir.

I was about to reply him, but a voice stopped me from behind. 'Are you Samarth?' asked a man who I think was in his 30s and wore a funky t-shirt and torn jeans.

'Yes,' I replied, bemused over the fact that an unknown person knew my name.

'Take this and do according to the instructions given to you,' said the man and he handed over the bags to me.

'How do you know me?' I asked.

'Don't waste your time,' he said to me and soon he was nowhere to be seen in the crowd.

'Why does nobody tell us the details?' asked Mihir.

As we started walking, we saw four police officers who were checking the station premises. My heart was in my mouth as I feared that the secret of the bag was about to be disclosed.

'I think this checking purpose is due to yesterday's blast,' said Aarav.

'I too think so,' I said.

We four stopped and didn't move for a while. We started discussing about what could be done to get past them.

'Boys!' a voice shouted.

It was one of the policemen and my heart almost stopped.

'Turn around,' I said to my brothers. 'Now, take out your handkerchiefs and cover your face,' I instructed.

Slowly the policemen walked towards us; we were all sweating from fear and there was only one way visible in front of me.

'Run,' I shouted, and we ran with the bags. Soon, we could hear the blowing of mouth whistles all over the station. The policemen started following us. We started climbing the stairs and running over the flyover and reached the main platform.

'Stop there!' said a loud voice from behind which indicated they were still following us.

While running, Aarav collided with a coolie and he fell down. I stopped and went back to help him out while the coolie hurled abuse at us. We continued our running and reached the main exit gate of the station. Now the running and the chasing round had hit the roads. We were running like scared pigs, sweating and breathing heavily.

'Catch them, don't let them go,' the voice still followed us. We ran, ran, and ran and soon reached a bus stop.

'Climb that bus,' I ordered.

'Are you mad?' asked Youhaan in a terrible voice.

'Run fast and get hold of the ladder behind the bus,' I said.

The bus had started moving and Aarav soon caught hold of the ladder. We started climbing the ladder quickly and reached the top.

'Stop the bus,' said the same voice. But it was too late for them to catch us; the bus was almost in its full flow. People everywhere were watching the roof of the bus astonishingly as if some criminals had escaped from jail.

'God, they treated us like criminals,' said Mihir as he lay down helplessly and breathed heavily. My legs had started to ache, and I was having difficulty getting my breath back. It didn't feel right. I always knew the kind of feeling I get when something happens out of adversity, but that day it seemed different. We felt like being a part of an evil force.

The four of us lay on top of the moving bus and looked up at the blue sky. We did not feel the cold as we were warmed up from our running. Time ran like an ostrich at a speed of about 70 km/h and we didn't know that in the coming few hours, we were going to have the biggest upset of our life. I peeked slightly to see where we had reached. The police officers were still following us in a jeep. They had initially lost some time in finding and tracking the route of the bus but were back in action.

'Guys, we still are in danger,' I said softly. All the three got tensed while I continued, 'keep your faces covered.'

The officers again started shouting, 'Stop the bus immediately.' This time the driver heard it too. I looked around and saw that the bus was slowing down for its first stop.

'Jump!' I said.

'What?'

'The bus is slowing down, and this is the right time, jump now,' I said.

Without wasting much time, the four of us jumped down one by one and started running. Seeing us escape, the officers ordered the jeep to stop and began to chase us again. While we were running, Aarav again collided with someone, but this time it was a person we never expected to see. It was Prithvi!

'Aarav, don't stop,' I said, while I came running towards him. Aarav had blundered, his handkerchief was no longer covering his face. Scared now, I pulled Aarav's hand and started running again. We both ran past, looking at Prithvi with our clueless faces.

'There's a car at the corner, look,' instructed Youhaan when we were almost giving up. 'Let's hide behind it.'

We quickly reached the car and placed ourselves comfortably behind it, in a position where no one could see us. I peeped through the window pane and saw the officers looking here and around for us.

'I think they headed straight,' said one of them.

'Let's move,' said another and they began to run again.

'Phewww...I think this time we have done it,' I said boosting up everyone.

'Thank God,' said Mihir.

'Let's wait for five minutes and after that, we will straight away head to the school,' I said.

'Not again. I don't have any stamina left to jump those walls,' said Youhaan who was in a terrible state. We could do nothing. We were there by our choice, so we had to move on. For a moment I thought, 'What is happening? Is this our life or some movie? Are we correct in what we are doing?' The last thought again haunted me for a minute. The fear killing me inside was about what the reaction would be back home. I didn't have any reply in store for the questions that would have been stored for us by now and my watch showed it was already 12 noon. Even though I might be successful in mollifying Di with our fake reasons, I had no idea what Prithvi would do. I only had one question in my mind...*would he have his revenge?*

The Paradise

Paradise was a synonym for heaven, but still, it had a deeper meaning. It was George, one of my classmates, who made me understand a different sense of it while standing in the assembly line of my school.

'When Jesus was on the cross,' said George, explaining to me an essential part of the Holy Bible, 'there were two thieves who were hanged along with him. One of them realized that Jesus was the son of God, and he begged for mercy and pardon for making fun of him. On hearing this, Jesus said to him: Today you will be with me in Paradise.'

Paradise is a place where God dwells. I believed it until I learned about Aastha Di's perception of it, which was quite a revelation for me.

'Di, why don't you get married?' I asked Aastha Di once when Delhi was facing one of its hottest summers. We were both lying on the floor on a mattress, surviving another hot day.

'I don't want to leave this paradise of ours,' said Di, showing her sentimental attachment to the place. But I was not in agreement with what she said. Why would she give this place an exaggerated name? There were cobwebs, seemingly uninhabited, hanging from the ceiling and over the wooden shelves. Some doors creaked as it opened, the windowpanes had a few tough stains developed over time, and the ceilings keep flaking off paint that had turned brittle. And dust, Aastha Di always had a tough time cleaning up the vast amount of dust that got accumulated inside.

'Are you serious?' I asked.

'Of course,' she said, ruffling my hair. 'I'm happy here with Aarav, Mihir, Youhaan, and you. You all are my children, and I built this place for you on my own. How can I abandon it?'

'But this is nowhere near to a paradise,' I said, almost breaking her heart.

'You think it's a place where you find luxury?' she asked smilingly. Before I could agree to her, she continued, 'For me, it's an idea. A place where I am safe and happy. This old house is our paradise. We're happy here, and we're safe.'

'That's true,' I said, agreeing to her last line. 'We shall always remain safe and happy here.'

'Promise me,' said Aastha Di, opening her palm. 'Promise me that you'll never do anything that compromises the safety of this place.'

'I promise,' I said.

I was sleeping on my bed when all these thoughts bobbed up in my consciousness. I was exhausted and so were my brothers, after the long chase. We had reached home by 2:00 pm after completing the job and slept till 6:00 pm. We again successfully placed those bags in the school without having to deal with any headache. Mihir was somehow right; I was good at giving excuses. I told Di that we were stuck in middle of a long and packed traffic jam and she was easily convinced.

'Today, we escaped by a whisker,' I said to myself. I slowly started to get out of my bed and found that my brothers were missing. I was walking out of my room when suddenly someone called me from outside. When I peeked outside the window, I saw Di and my brothers standing along with a crowd of people.

'Now what's the matter?' I asked to myself and started walking downstairs.

When I reached down my breath almost stopped. It felt like someone had pulled me down forcefully from my world of dreams to the harsh reality. I saw in front of me, Di standing with an angry look on her face, my brothers with their lips trembling out of fear, Aradhna Di and the girls giving me surprised looks, the crowd chattering away as usual and two police officers with sticks in their hands. I was terrified looking at this view.

'Are you Samarth?' asked one policeman, suddenly appearing in front of me.

'Ummm... yes,' I replied hesitatingly.

'I am Kishen Singh, the area inspector,' he replied, which stopped my senses. 'I am checking and enquiring about all the boys in this locality. We have seen some boys covering their faces and running with some bags around India Gate and New Delhi Railway Station.'

'I am not among them, sir,' I replied foolishly, out of frustration.

'Neither had I said that,' he said, turning towards his colleague. 'Bring that boy here,' he ordered, and I was wondering whom he was calling.

But very soon, our fate had reached its inevitable end; the boy he called was none other than Prithvi. It was easy for me to guess why he was brought here.

'Is it him? Whom you saw hours ago?' asked the officer.

My heart started thumping faster as if it would come out in a minute. Prithvi thought for a while and said, 'No, sir.'

I heaved a sigh of relief. But at the same time, I was confused. Why hadn't he disclosed my name? If he had seen Aarav, then it would not have been difficult at all for him to guess who the other three were.

'Okay, let's move further,' he said, and moved towards my brothers. They were already in a state of nervous breakdown and could not handle even a little pressure.

'Is it him?' he asked, pointing towards Mihir.

Prithvi again denied it and he did the same when he was asked to recognize Youhaan.

'He's the last one. Think carefully,' said the officer, pointing his finger towards Aarav. I was dead. Aarav was the only person whose face Prithvi had seen. Prithvi looked at Aarav sharply. There was a long silence as Prithvi paused for a moment. I remembered the words he had uttered that day... 'There will be a day, the day when I'll give you a big shock. The shock will make you bewildered.' I didn't need to get a Ph.D. to conclude that he'd surely have his revenge this time. His day had begun and ours was ending.

'G-O-D,' I spelled silently as he was about to deliver his answer. My Paradise was in danger.

A New Beginning

'What if I had a magic clock?' I thought while standing in the assembly line. The holidays were finally over, and we were back in school. It might be due to my principal's speech on time management that got me into a realm of fantasy for a moment.

'What if I had a magic clock, and I could roll back time to whichever point I wanted,' I still continued thinking. 'Apart from trying to change the course of time, I would go and revisit my past when things were unfair to me.'

Our principal moved forward towards the edge of the stage and continued with his speech. 'Dear students,' he said, 'you will be a master of your life if you learn to design a timetable for yourself.'

As he continued speaking, I dwelt further into my daydream. I wished if I could move back the hands of the clock to that day when I started hating Prithvi. I could've changed a few moments that inflicted strong dislikes in me for him. I could've made him my friend a long ago. Keeping an apology letter in my shirt pocket that I had written to Prithvi, expressing my sincere regret, I looked for him everywhere. I needed to talk to him badly, but he was nowhere to be seen.

'Are you looking for Prithvi?' asked Aarav during the assembly.

'You too?' I asked.

'Yes,' he replied hesitatingly.

I was feeling very clumsy and maladroit as I was attending school after so many days. The second day of the New Year was far more pleasant, but my mind wasn't. After a dangerous first day, I hoped this day would pass without any difficulty. I saw the other students standing and yawning in the assembly line. They had to reset their wake-up timings because they had lost the habit of waking up early. Thanks to our jogging, we didn't have that problem.

'Ending my speech on a positive note,' said our principal, 'I welcome you all to a new year of aspirations and excellence. Hope you all enjoyed your winter vacations. Now, it's time to get back to business. It's time to study since your exams are about to start in ten days.'

'Ten days? That's not fair,' I said, finding his decision as inhuman. I badly needed some magical powers to change that count to a year.

Soon, our assembly was dismissed, and we went straight to our classes. I was still looking for Prithvi.

'Wow! We are going to sleep so early,' said Mihir after finding that the first period was of English. I didn't bother to reply him because I was in search of some inner peace. I took the apology letter in my hands, opened it and started reading its contents.

Dear Prithvi,

We don't even have the right to seek an apology from you for what we have done to you in the past. But today, we are on the right path and look forward to extend a hand of unending friendship with you. To help us move forward, can you please forgive all of us wholeheartedly? It would be so great if you join our group and share our world. With open arms we welcome you to become a part of our family.

If you accept our apology, meet us on the stage, we'll be waiting for you.

Samarth

'Why is he late?' I said to myself as I folded back the letter.

'Sir, may I come in?' I heard a voice suddenly from the classroom door and I saw Prithvi standing with his bag. I was quite relaxed after seeing him. For what he had done for us was something extraordinary.

'Why so late?' asked Narayan Sir.

'Had some emergency, sir.'

We were obliged to him for his greatness. He saved our paradise; he preserved the remaining happiness of our family. Seeing him enter the classroom, I remembered the last evening, the evening of New Year's Day:

'I think we should move on, he is not the one whom we are looking for,' said Prithvi, when he was asked to recognize Aarav. I couldn't believe my ears, my senses started working, and my heart started pumping blood again. I believed that I was still alive, and my frustration levels dropped down. Even Aarav couldn't believe what had happened. Di had a look of relief on her face and the crowd started moving away as nothing much seemed to be happening. The girls on the balcony were also relieved. Prithvi started moving back, seeing Aarav's relieved look. How could someone be so kind and forgiving after going through such a long series of humiliations?

'Sorry for the disturbance,' said the inspector.

The officers started moving, giving me a furious look. Prithvi had an innocent look on his face with a sign of satisfaction that he had done something good. He was someone who had a pure heart and matured thinking. He didn't have any problem with us. Whatever problems were created were due to our egos and under-aged mentality.

'Why does everyone have a misunderstanding with us?' I said to Di, to lighten the situation.

'Thank God it was just a doubt, otherwise I would have killed you.'

I swallowed some saliva into my throat after hearing those words from her. Soon the area was cleared; the crowd was back to their routine business. We started moving up towards our home in a relaxed way, but my mind was full of thoughts about Prithvi. It was not anything less than a miracle that had happened in front of me.

Amid an interesting lesson from my English textbook about Ebenezer Scrooge and the three ghosts of Christmas, I folded the letter neatly and threw it towards Prithvi, who was sitting in the adjacent row. The paper fell on his desk and he looked at me, surprised. I indicated to him with my action that he should read it. At first, he didn't bother and kept it in between his book. When the third period of physics was going on, I saw him taking out the paper from his book and unfolding it. I looked at him till he completed reading my letter. He looked at me with an expressionless face after reading it which made me sad, but still I hoped for the best. Soon the bell rang for lunch and the students were running outside like wild bulls.

'So hungry I am, let's go,' said Mihir highly excited.

'Shut up! We have some work, come with me,' I said.

We came outside our classroom to the open grounds were students were having their lunch. There one could see large circles of friends sitting and having their tiffin, some taking stuff from the canteen, and some couples having a walk.

'Is Avni coming to meet you?' asked Mihir.

'No, I'll meet her later,' I replied as I placed myself on the stage.

'Then?'

'It's Prithvi,' I replied, finally breaking the suspense.

'Good job bro, even I wanted to meet him,' said Youhaan smilingly.

'Are you both mad?' asked Mihir.

'Look Mihir, we were always wrong about Prithvi,' I said, making him understand the gravity of the situation. 'What he did for us, I don't think anyone else would have done that. He saved Aarav from the law; he saved our Di's dignity and respect, and our reputation in the school. Can you imagine a worse situation if he would have said 'yes' at that time?'

Mihir was quiet for some time; he was deeply touched hearing my words. When we looked straight ahead, we saw the girls in front of us, standing at a distance. We were happy that the holidays were over and now we could talk to them freely with no time limit or restrictions. When we were about to call them on stage, a voice stopped us.

'Someone called me?'

When we turned back to see who it was, I could not control my happiness. We stood up seeing Prithvi in front of us and looked at him calmly. Aarav walked towards him as we watched him silently. He hugged him at once. I could no longer believe my eyes. I never imagined this kind of a day where we would enjoy Prithvi's presence around us. We three ran towards them and hugged them even more tightly and started shouting madly.

'Let me breathe, guys,' said Prithvi.

'I am so happy that you forgave us,' I said.

'My mother says if you do not forgive a person for his mistakes, you are taking away his only chance of reconciliation,' said Prithvi.

His mother was right. If Prithvi wouldn't have forgiven us, we would have never been enraptured in this beautiful moment. Where our hatred always maligned his pure nature, our likeness will surely put an end to all the hostilities between us.

'Hey, I am sorry for whatever I did to you,' said Aarav, expressing his sorrow. 'I don't know why I did all those things.'

'In fact, none of us knows why we were like that to you,' said Mihir.

'Now forget it, I don't have any complaints,' said Prithvi. 'But I need to say one thing—Mihir, I am sorry for kicking your stomach twice that day.'

We all had a good laugh after hearing that. It was good to see Prithvi getting along so well with us. Though Prithvi didn't needed a formal introduction, I decided to introduce him to Avni and the other girls.

'Prithvi, your new friend?' said Avni, disbelieving the truth standing in front of her. I was not at all surprised by her reaction as she would've never thought we could befriend our biggest foe.

'You need to believe this, we have sorted out all our differences,' said Aarav, ensuring all of them about the good change that happened inside all of us.

'That's good,' said Tamanna. Her face was still dull and gloomy. She was not looking at Aarav to his face, and he was the same emotionless person. His nature seemed to be changing from time to time.

'In addition to a new member, I think you all need to change your group's name a little bit,' said Suhaani.

'Yes, we'll think of it,' I said.

'You all share such good chemistry,' said Prithvi, enjoying the camaraderie between all of us. 'I am lucky to be with you all.'

'We are lucky to have you as one of our friends,' said Avni. Her words brought him into a happy state. It seemed that he had finally filled up that empty void of his life. For a boy who had spent almost his entire school life without friends, it was nirvana.

'Well, can we celebrate this new friendship?' asked Prithvi.

'No, it's not possible, I think you know our family background,' I said. All of us wanted to say 'yes' for a party but couldn't.

'Yes, I know it. But don't worry, I'll talk to your sisters,' said Prithvi.

'No, don't do that, it will be terrible,' said Avni.

'She is right,' I said, in support of her.

'Don't worry, I have a plan,' said Prithvi.

I thought he was joking until he stood at our doorstep on the same day in the evening. Aastha Di had a new visitor on that day, a stranger who she didn't know would become an integral part of her family.

'With your permission shall I take them out for some time?' asked Prithvi politely and eating the cookies served to him. Di examined him as if he was an alien visitor on earth. Nobody from school had ever knocked at our door asking to spend quality time with us.

'I am not comfortable in sending them along with Avni and the others,' said Aastha Di, giving an answer we had expected from her.

'I understand, Di,' said Prithvi. 'But surprisingly, Aradhna Di doesn't seem to have any problem in allowing the girls to spend some time with us.'

Our mouths nearly fell open on hearing his words, but more than us, it was Aastha Di whose ego melted like wax from a burning candle. She could never step back after learning that her younger sister was so down-to-earth in this matter. We knew Prithvi was lying but his words had hit the nail on the head.

'Fine,' said Aastha Di, considering changing her decision. 'But just one hour. They all should be back by then.'

The four of us felt a dramatic revolution happening in that room. Though driven by sheer self-respect, Aastha Di's answer had indicated a change in time. The power of her approval was not less than my imaginary magic clock. I took away three crucial learnings from that day. First, even good people like Prithvi lied, and second, it is okay to lie, but the purpose behind it should have nothing but pure intentions. The third one was the one I feared the most. The way Prithvi managed to change Aastha Di's mind reminded me of Iqbal. What if we were mistaken about him and were failing to see through his clever manipulations? What if he had made us believe something which he was not?

An Evening to Remember

We reached CP in approximately 15 minutes, thanks to that rickshaw driver who was so quick. CP, or Connaught Place, is one of the largest financial, commercial, and business centres in Delhi named after the Duke of Connaught. We were in the beautiful Central Park. The sun was almost setting and was scattering its magnificent light all over the horizon. The scene was making the park even more beautiful.

'You guys take a walk around inside, it will be fun,' said Prithvi, which astonished me. 'It's been years since you all are in a relationship and you haven't gone for a date till now.'

An hour ago, I was stupefied when Prithvi convinced Aradhna Di in the same way he had convinced Aastha Di. He showed me that being egoistic was a bad thing and how people can use your own ego against you. This time I was astounded when he said that he took all that pain so that four of us could spend a few romantic moments with our respective partners.

'Listen, it's not working at all,' I said, finding his thoughts and ideas as unreal. Not even a day into his new friendship, he had started doing many things for us. It wouldn't be wrong to say that I had a twinge of doubt about his intentions, but it was also true that I had started overthinking, especially after that harrowing incident at the railway station. Even standing in that park, I was having an uncanny feeling of being watched.

'It will work, give it a try,' said Prithvi.

'Then what will you do?'

'Don't worry about me...you guys have a nice time. This place is appropriate for a romantic walk. Just be aware of the time.'

'But Prithvi,' interrupted Tamanna who was feeling awkward that she had to spend some alone time with Aarav.

'It's okay,' said Prithvi and he started walking away. 'We only have one hour. I will be in that restaurant there.'

We saw Prithvi giving all of us a thumbs up. I remembered those days around our annual day function when once, we had shown thumbs down to him. He was something else, something out of this world. I was wondering what material his heart was made of.

'I wish time would freeze right here,' said Avni, resting her head on my shoulder. We all were having a nice time together inside the Park. Avni and I were sitting in front of the Amphitheatre.

'It's so beautiful, you and this silence around us,' I said.

'Samarth,' said Avni, holding me more tightly. 'For the first time you are this close to me.'

'And I don't want it to be the last time.'

As soon as I said this, she looked towards me with her natural elegance. At that time I felt as if violins were playing around me. I felt as if her eyes were the lyrics of the tune and her smile provided the vocals.

'What happened?' she asked me suddenly.

'I feel as if I am seeing your eyes for the first time,' I replied, and she came closer to me. Close enough to listen to my heartbeats and close enough to listen to the breath of my soul. Though this public display of affection made me uncomfortable, I was sinking in the moment. When I gave a look towards the other side, I saw Mihir and Sandhya too were sitting in front of the amphitheatre. They were admiring the beautiful evening around them in their own way.

Youhaan and Suhaani were sitting in front of the fountain and enjoying the coloured water coming out of it; they might have seen those colours in each other's eyes. That fountain might have taken them to the time when they both proposed to each other. It was not easy for them to forget that moment.

One autumn, they both bunked during school time and headed to the Purana Qila. Bunking school was wrong and for a studious girl like Suhaani to do so was out of the ordinary, so strong was the power of love. Purana Qila is the inner citadel of the city of Din-panah, founded by Humayun. Youhaan and Suhaani entered through the Bara Darwaza, the Big Gate, facing West, one among the three gates of the fort. They both took a walk inside the premises of the fort holding each other's hands for a while. They finally sat on a shallow tank which once had a beautiful fountain. Youhaan took out a medium sized diary from his bag and handed it over to Suhaani.

'Open it,' he said.

She opened it with full excitement and very soon was on cloud nine when she viewed the pictures inside it. The diary contained the most angelic and beauteous photographs of Suhaani, pasted creatively by Youhaan. Each page she turned and found herself more beautiful. Her smile was hugging her lips during the time she was lost in the diary. When she reached the last page, there was no photograph, but a line written on it - Look in front.

When she obeyed the words of that line, she found Youhaan sitting in front of her on his knees.

'You're more beautiful than your pictures,' said Youhaan. 'Will you say yes if I say that we both are unconditionally in love with each other?'

'Of course, I will say 'yes', stupid,' replied Suhaani blissfully, and with that 'yes' started a beautiful relationship between a bookworm and a photographer. Time was merely an accessory for them and the people around just a distraction which they could ignore easily. They were giving the world a challenge...find us if you can. They spent their remaining hours boating in a lake adjacent to Purana Qila.

I wanted to spend the rest of my life in that park reminiscing about the past. When I looked around, I could hear the birds chirping our old tales and the leaves rustling in the wind about our delightful times. Aastha Di was right. Your paradise is a place where you're safe and happy. The thought about Aastha Di suddenly reminded me about our time limit.

'Get up, we need to go,' I said, standing up and helping Avni to stand up.

I saw Aarav at some distance, walking in front of Tamanna like a king who had lost his empire. Tamanna was watching him pessimistically and cynically. She threw a small stone at him to disturb him. Her act demonstrated her cuteness. Aarav looked at her, astonished. He stared at her for a moment and then walked towards the exit gate of the park to find a rickshaw. Tamanna was trying to lighten the awkward situation that was developing but he couldn't understand it.

We all straightaway headed to the restaurant where Prithvi had told us to meet. When we entered inside, we were surprised to see him sitting along with Radhika and her sister Meera. He was completely lost in Radhika as she was smiling beautifully at him.

'Hey, guys,' said Prithvi after seeing us standing at the entrance of the restaurant. 'So, how was it?'

'Truly, we will never forget this one,' said Youhaan. It was written on all of our faces that we had a mesmerizing evening.

'Well, she's Radhika,' said Prithvi, introducing her to us. It was the first time I was watching Radhika closely. I've always been a silent observer in her case, and I could proudly say that Prithvi and Radhika were made for each other. It was not because they looked nice together but because they completed each other.

'Prithvi, it's time, we need to go. I think we are already late,' warned Avni.

'I think you guys will make home, I need to drop Meera and Radhika to their home,' said Prithvi.

'Absolutely no problem, we can make it,' I said.

'Listen Prithvi, bring Radhika to our home whenever you get time,' said Avni.

'Of course,' said Prithvi.

We started moving from there, saying goodbye to all. We walked out of the park within a few minutes through the exit gate. The time we were out, we were back on business—that is, looking for a rickshaw. The evening began to get darker and colder. The icy cold killed the romance that had prevailed inside the park. Tamanna was standing still near the roadside, thinking of something very deeply. She may have been thinking of the awkward time spent with Aarav inside the park. It was really hard for her to spend time with a guy who didn't bother to give her the much-deserved attention. She was still thinking very deeply when her mind got diverted and she looked the other side. The scene was exactly as if her thoughts had become reality. She saw Aarav getting out of a rickshaw and then looking towards her. They both looked at each other and she felt as if she was hearing a voice, a voice she had heard for years, a voice that has always encouraged her to love Aarav. The voice of her own soul.

'Hey guys, I got one,' shouted Aarav towards us. He then looked at Tamanna for the second time. He saw her walking towards him like a princess who had crossed every boundary set by her family just to meet her love. Her hair was dancing to the calm and silent whistle of the breeze. That must have made his heart go for a roller-coaster ride, but he wouldn't show that on his face. Only a short distance was left between both of them when something terrible happened. The disgusting chain snatchers struck again. Sitting on their fast bikes and accelerating to a level that made them fly in the air, they snatched Tamanna's chain from her neck. They were off after that, so quickly that we couldn't understand what had happened. As they snatched her chain, she lost her balance and was about to fall when a hand held her tightly. That hand helped her to regain her balance and she was alright.

'Thank...' she said her half sentence and stopped by looking at the person standing in front of her. The person was none other than Aarav himself.

'Are you alright?' asked Aarav, to which Tamanna didn't reply anything.

By that time, we all came running and shouting at those chain snatchers. We panicked because of what we saw in front of us just a moment ago.

'Are you okay, dear?' asked Sandhya in a flash.

'Yes...I am fine,' said Tamanna.

'I can't believe these senseless guys,' said Youhaan, bringing out his anger.

While we were talking, Aarav noticed that Tamanna was bleeding a little bit from the side of her neck.

'You're bleeding,' he shouted, which stunned everyone. Avni quickly checked and said, 'Oh! God!'

But what Aarav did after that stunned us even more. He took out his handkerchief and started wiping the blood slowly as if it was he who was bleeding. I could clearly see the reflection of her pain in his eyes. Seeing that, I wondered...how could he be so stubborn with his heart? Tamanna knew that he had this capability of absorbing everyone's pain, maybe that was why she silently observed him. But before her silence could prevail for longer, she ended it herself.

'Stop it Aarav, it's just a scratch,' she said.

'But it's bleeding.'

'You don't worry about that, I am fine.'

Tamanna was angry with him and that was the reason she was again and again harsh on him. And I was sure about the fact that he didn't like it.

'Let's get home quickly now,' I said.

We were able to find a second rickshaw as eight people could not be accommodated in one. We started our journey back home, leaving behind the beautiful Central Park and a few priceless moments. What was still in its place was the puzzling love story of Aarav and Tamanna. Avni and I were sitting along with them in one rickshaw. All my attention was on Aarav. I was trying to read his mind, but I couldn't. Tamanna was silently watching the scenario outside the auto, rushing past her in the opposite direction. Maybe those scenarios showed her that lovely future in which she and her love lived in a house near the shallow waters, or maybe back in her favourite place, Kashmir, where they would enjoy the colourful upland birds flying in the Pahalgam skyline, or maybe the snowy lanes of Sonamarg.

Soon, our short journey ended, and we were back where we belonged to. We stopped the rickshaw some distance away from our home to avoid any further punishment. We paid the driver and decided to walk as we always did, faking a feeling of hatred for each other. Within a few minutes, we were in the middle of those two buildings and started going in opposite directions. But we stopped after hearing a voice.

'Take care, Tamanna,' said Aarav and he started climbing the stairs.

Tamanna watched him for a few minutes with deep, sad eyes. That was enough for her, those three words became her life. We all had had the evening of our lifetime which had become our most beautiful memory. Talking about Prithvi, he had entered our lives with a bang. If he hadn't planned this evening, we would have missed watching the real Aarav, we could have missed how the universe plans each love story. Prithvi did not have a single element of hatred in his heart for us and it was like he was gifting happy memories to us. I didn't know about the others, but I was excited to live the coming days of my life. I was excited to see what more miracles Prithvi would create in our paradise.

Exam Fever

'One, two, three and jump,' I said, as we stood in front of Prithvi's bed, on which he was taking his afternoon nap peacefully. We jumped on him like a cheetah jumping on its delicious prey. He woke up suddenly, freaking out at high pitch and we laughed like mad boys.

'What the hell?' asked Prithvi, half sleeping and rubbing his eyes.

'We thought we'd give you a surprise,' said Youhaan.

'Don't try to fool me,' he said, yawning on the bed. 'I am not your girlfriend that you would love to give me a surprise.'

Prithvi was a smart guy. It was easy for him to figure out the purpose of our paying him a visit suddenly on a Sunday afternoon. Though an immodest thing to admit, yes, our visit was purely on selfish grounds. We were here to ask something that we never asked in our life.

'Just give me 10 minutes, I'll freshen up and come,' said Prithvi.

We waited for him in the bedroom, looking at and admiring the walls which were creatively painted. We saw a big poster of Bryan Adams hanging from the wall and Prithvi's guitar rested against it. Prithvi was fond of music but I never had a chance to listen to him because of the unfriendly circumstances that had prevailed between us. And, trust me, listening to some soulful songs was the medicine I needed for the feeling of uneasiness in me. Even though I looked cool and calm, I was melting rapidly from inside with trepidation. Just seven days were left for our exams and we didn't even dare to open our books. Tension was slowly mounting in me.

'Waiting for me?' asked Prithvi suddenly, entering with a tray of cups filled with coffee. 'Hot coffee for a cold day,' he said, as he offered the cups one by one. He sat on the sofa holding a cup for himself and continued, 'Now tell, what help do you want from me?'

'I want you to tutor me for my exams,' I said, coming straight to the point. 'I am equivalent to a big zero when it comes to studies.'

'Only this much?' asked Prithvi, taking a sip of the coffee. 'This is not a big deal.'

'You mean you will help me?'

'Why only you? I will help you all.'

I liked people who had surety in their words. Prithvi's words always played somewhere between confidence and overconfidence. He spoke from the heart. For a person like me, who believed that the most illogical decisions come from the heart, I was compelled to change my thought.

'Thank you,' I said to him.

'It's okay,' he said. 'When Avni approached me today for some help in studies, she spoke about you. I think she knew you would be stressed.'

I smiled for a moment after hearing that.

'But I need to know something,' said Prithvi. His tone caused my expression to change. 'Why were those police officers chasing you that day?'

I felt the ground beneath me shaking. I had no idea what to answer. Staring at him, I felt like standing at the crossroads of my life. Either I could tell him some lies and get away or I could tell him the truth and respect our blossoming friendship. And, I chose the latter.

'We four are part of a secret mission,' I replied to him.

'What type of mission?' he asked, and I told him whatever had happened, each and every turn in the story. He was not the kind of person whom we could fool easily.

'I still can't believe you,' he said, reacting as if the coffee was too hot for him to hold. 'Are you sure about this man?'

'Yes, we are quite sure. He seems like an army man to me based on his appearance and behaviour. It's time we do something for our country.'

'I remember this man,' said Prithvi. 'I was there when he stopped all of us from fighting that day.' He stood up and took his guitar which was nicely resting against the wall. It sounded a bit out of tune when he played a few random chords. 'Somehow, I don't think you are on the right path,' he said as he started tuning it by hearing the pitch of each string, starting from the sixth one.

'You guys are not at all aware of the world outside there, are you? Doing something for your country is brilliant but it is important you choose the right path. Moreover, I don't think the army requires help from kids like us. They will never allow common citizens to indulge in dangerous ventures.'

As Prithvi progressed on each string, we felt as if it was us who were getting tuned by his words and not the guitar. I had the same feeling of being enmeshed in a tawdry business sitting on the top of the bus that day while escaping from the cops. But at that moment, any decision taken by me would not have been a well-thought one. I decided to give it some time until we backed out entirely from Iqbal and his project. Patience, it was time for me to implement what I learned.

'Don't worry, we have a little faith in ourselves,' I said smilingly.

'And this is the first reward we got,' said Mihir, taking out the mobile phone from his pocket.

'How did you get that?' asked Prithvi, keeping aside his guitar.

'We got Rs. 10,000 when we completed our first job. We bought the phone with that money. In fact, we bought it today itself, while coming to your home,' I replied.

'It's among the best cellular phones,' said Mihir, kissing the mobile.

'But I am getting some negative vibes from it,' said Prithvi with a weird look. 'I think you should throw it away as quickly as possible.'

'You think so much, just relax,' said Aarav after feeling that he was getting too negative.

'I must think because it's about you all, it's about your safety,' said Prithvi. 'I believe it's some kind of a trap. You all should be careful.'

I could see a pessimistic observer in Prithvi. I couldn't understand why he was so morbid about a mobile phone. But at the same time, I didn't completely ignore his point of view. As far as I knew, he wouldn't be hyper about something unless he was absolutely sure.

'Just calm down, we are all perfectly safe,' said Youhaan.

'And yes, please don't tell Di about our secret work,' I said.

'I won't. But still, I recommend you should share this with your sister,' said Prithvi.

'We will when it's time,' I said, completing my cup of coffee.

The seven days left for the exams to begin were now reduced to just six days and we were at the beginning stage of our studies. But I was happy because now, we had started studying. We managed to open our books and go through the syllabus. It all happened because of Prithvi and the strict schedule that he imposed on us. He decided that he would teach us every day from 3:00 pm to 8:00 pm after school. He was strict like Narayan Sir, but we loved and enjoyed his company and teaching. We four sat in our room with our Physics textbook opened in front of us. Prithvi, our teacher for the evening, had instructed us to start with the most important unit in Physics, ray and wave optics.

'When a beam of light strikes the water,' said Prithvi, explaining to us the concept of total internal reflection, 'a part of light is reflected while some part is refracted.'

He explained the laws of physics to us , but we related it to Prithvi's natural reactions. His concentration was like that beam of light. It was divided between us and the things happenings in the opposite building. Prithvi had brought Radhika to Avni's home, fulfilling his promise. Since then, he could hardly keep his mind steady. He opened his English textbook and tried reading it attentively. Everything was going very fine; the atmosphere around us had become studious, and soon we were enjoying the art of studying for the first time. We were well able to understand what each line of our textbook meant. We consulted Prithvi whenever we were obstructed with a doubt. But soon, our enjoyment was disturbed with the sounds of a quarrel.

'I think someone is fighting,' said Prithvi.

'Yes, it's from the ground floor, Mr. and Mrs. Desai,' I said, looking at the wall clock which showed 7:30 pm.

'It's too disturbing, especially at this time,' said Prithvi.

'We can do nothing, it's their routine,' said Mihir.

'Tell me something about them that you know,' said Prithvi, closing his textbook and diverting his mind to an altogether different topic.

'We don't know much about them,' said Youhaan, 'just a little, based on what Di told us.'

'Alright, tell me that,' said Prithvi.

'Well, Mr. Desai is a retired army man. He fell in love with Mrs. Desai when they both were neighbours in Ahmedabad. Being the victims of love at first sight, they had a love marriage.'

'Yes,' supported Aarav and he continued further. 'Mr. Desai is a big fan of the legendary actor Mr. Manoj Kumar and his patriotic movies. It is due to his films that he decided to join the army. He was that much inspired.'

'Mr. Desai,' I said, continuing the narrative, 'often took her to watch movies secretly without informing either of the families. Most of the time they used to watch only the great patriotic movies of that time. The first movie they watched together was *Purab aur Paschim.*'

'They both married even though their families had objections. Di told us that they escaped at midnight and from there, they started their long, married life. But I never saw any love between them except when Mr. Desai had a heart attack recently,' said Mihir, completing the story.

'Hmmm...now I get it,' said Prithvi, who seemed to have reached a conclusion from our inputs. 'From the perspective of a school boy, I can infer that it's a case where partners disagree with each other's opinion.'

We had no clue how he could derive that wisdom from the bits and pieces of the story that we offered. We listened to him further. 'Problems arise in this type of situation and it's quite natural. It happens often in love marriages when both partners fail to keep the promises which they had taken before the marriage. You all must be thinking how I know this?'

He had very well read the big question mark on each of our faces and said, 'My cousin brother ended his married life in only four years. It was a similar kind of a situation. Unfortunately, he and his wife couldn't bear the burden of a failed marriage for long.' Ending with a sad note, Prithvi took out two pages from a notebook.

'What are you going to do?' I asked.

'I'll tell you soon,' he said and started to write something on the pages. I have heard about people who were born with extraordinary minds. It would not be an exaggeration for me to say that Prithvi had an extraordinary mind. What we could not understand all these years in spite of knowing things, he could figure out in a few minutes. His remarkable ability to stick to the basics always impressed me.

Soon it was 8:00 pm and we completed three-fourths of the unit. We were feeling very satisfied with our work as it was the first time that we had studied for five hours continuously, that too without eating anything. Di came into our room and asked if we wanted to eat something, but we refused. We closed our textbooks and started doing some stretching to convey how hard we'd been working.

'Relax till dinner,' said Prithvi, seeing us.

'What were you writing all this time?' asked Aarav.

'Letters,' said Prithvi, which surprised us. And, even before we asked about the recipients, he said, 'to the lovers, Mr. and Mrs. Desai.'

It surprised us even more. We saw a great excitement in Prithvi that he was about to do something good. It reminded me of the priest's words about the necessity of sustaining goodness in the world.

'I can't understand,' said Youhaan, asking for some more explanation.

'You will; come with me,' said Prithvi and we followed him. I had a doubt that he was again going to show some miracle, so I called Di along with us. I thought she should also have the joy of watching the impossible being converted to the possible. We all reached downstairs, following Prithvi and stopped right in front of Desai Uncle's door.

Prithvi slowly opened the bedroom window and saw Aunty sitting on the bed.

'Prithvi, it's bad manners,' said Di in a soft voice.

'Di, I am so sorry, but I have to do this,' he said and threw one of the letters inside the window and quickly closed it. Next, he went towards the scooter and placed the other letter on the back seat with a stone on it to keep it from falling off the scooter.

He knocked their door and then asked us to hide near one side of the staircase and observe the happenings. A moment later, we saw Desai Uncle coming out of the house. He could find no one but saw a letter kept on the back seat of his scooter. After reading it, he folded it back and looked towards the bedroom window. For the first time we saw a cute smile on his face. It was hard to believe that he could actually smile like that. We came out from our hiding place after seeing Desai uncle walking inside his house. Looking at his shy face, I could say with surety that he felt like a newly married man that day. Aradhna Di and the girls were observing the entire goings-on from the top, wondering what was happening.

'Di, I know it's bad manners, but I need to do this one more time,' said Prithvi and he opened the bedroom window once again. The view we saw inside left us all in a state of oblivion. We thought we were dreaming.

'Can someone pinch me?' asked Di after seeing Desai Aunty resting her head on her husband's shoulders. The scene was unbelievable, and we had no clue what Prithvi had done to make this happen. He slowly closed the window and said, 'I think now we should leave them to enjoy their special moments.'

'What did you do, Prithvi?' asked Di.

'Nothing Di, I just showed their misunderstandings an exit door and made them realize that they are living for each other,' said Prithvi.

No marriage is a perfect marriage. The beauty starts with all the imperfections. At our age it was hard to apprehend the implications of marriage on life, but I was sure about one thing. Out of all the imperfections of a married life there would always be one thing to cherish about—love. I was happy that I realized something more about it.

'But how?' asked Di, curious to know about the solution.

'I just wrote two simple letters for them, pretending that they have written it for each other,' said Prithvi and he narrated the contents of the letters to us. We all were smiling after hearing the contents of the letter.

'My dad taught me that the answers to all our questions are just hidden around us,' said Prithvi. 'They are invisible till we are desperate to find them.'

Di went to him with her beautiful smiling face, kissed his forehead and said, 'God bless you.'

That day, Aastha Di gave Prithvi a place in her paradise. After us, it took a decade for another kid to capture her heart. And, Prithvi was the most unexpected of all. But it was not over. There were others waiting for him.

'Prithvi, come upstairs,' shouted Avni, standing at the window. 'You know who's waiting for you, right?' We could understand what she meant by that and Prithvi was smiling.

'Di, I am sorry. I need to go now; I'll be back tomorrow,' said Prithvi. He quickly got his bag and books from our room and ran up the stairs of the other building. We were laughing at his innocence and enthusiasm. At the same time, the contents of the letters which he wrote were still circling around me.

I still remember the day when we both lied to our families and went out to watch Purab aur Paschim. You were looking beautiful, just like Saira Banu, and I watched you more than her. You remember how we held our hands when the song 'Koi Jab Tumhara Hriday' played on the screen? I think only we both understood the true soul of the song. We loved each other truly, but what has happened now? Why we are fighting like this? We need to end this. So, what if we've become a little old-fashioned today, we can still go and watch them and just relish and relive our old happy times. I want to do all those things which will bring your smiling face back. Please don't say anything about this letter to me; you know I still feel shy writing love letters.

Expecting a hug from you,

Your loving husband.

A brief, sweet, innocent and sensible letter had done the trick. He had written the second letter by changing a few words, bringing some femininity into it, and using the closing tag as - *Your loving wife.*

That night, after having dinner, I was watching the Venetian window of the front building where Prithvi was playing his guitar and Aradhna Di and the girls were sitting around him, clapping for the song he was singing. It was the same song that he always sung. The miracle man had just delivered another miracle that day, one worth remembering. We completed the unit which he had told us to do and were feeling very satisfied with our hard work. Suddenly, while relishing my small success, an interesting thought hit me. Mr. and Mrs. Desai could've easily found out that the letters were not written by either of them through the handwriting on the paper. But it didn't happen. It was proof that the eternal power called God governed every nook and cranny of the earth. His strong blessings were with Prithvi. Time, at last, proved me wrong. There was only one thing in this world today that ensured a happy living— goodness.

Lurking in the Darkness

Our school timings were changed to 9:00 am due to decreasing temperatures. In January, a dense fog enveloped the city, reducing visibility on the streets. I was happy thinking that now, I would be able to sleep for more hours on account of my late-night studies and secret meetings with Iqbal. Yes, I met him alone a few times in the dark hours of the night, purposely keeping my brothers out of it. I didn't want to drift them away from their peaceful phase. Iqbal's frustration was clearly visible as he was meeting me after many days.

'Are you saying to me that this can't be done?' asked Iqbal, standing at a corner of an empty street. We started having an argument when I didn't simply say 'yes' this time.

'All I am saying is it'll not be easy now,' I said, looking to my side to ensure that no one was hearing us. 'The school has re-opened after the holidays and is a bit busy at the moment.'

'This is the last time I'm asking you,' he said, raising his eyebrows. 'We need these remaining bags to be kept at the same place.'

His tone sounded forceful unlike the other times when it was convincing. 'Fine, give me some time. I'll come up with a plan.'

It was enough for him to leave me and walk away. I also gave him my phone number as an assurance that I'm always reachable. The look he gave before leaving seemed like a warning, but I ignored it. My head had started to feel heavy with everything and all I wanted was some sleep. But my dreams were shattered. My sleep got disturbed with Youhaan's loud snoring. I kicked his butt in anger, but still he didn't stop snoring. When I was finally irritated and start to get out of the bed, I got scared by the sight of Mihir sitting on his bed with his monkey cap on and a thermometer inside his mouth.

'It's been two days I am seeing you, why the hell do you scare me like this?' I asked him.

'With the exam days having arrived, I am feeling feverish. I need to consult a doctor,' he said.

'Yes, you really need to, but a mental doctor,' I replied.

We were about to start a serious conversation on Mihir's madness when we were stopped by a shout and thumping on the door.

All of you get up and do some revision!

It was 8:30 am and we were ready, waiting for our bus at the bus stop. For once, surprisingly, we had books in our hands, and we were revising whatever we had studied. Those days of slavery and bondage had arrived where we had only two companions, our textbooks and our anxieties. We were in a great panic situation, not because we were giving exams for the first time, but because we were giving exams after studying seriously. I understood why the other children looked petrified and scary with their red eyes on exam days.

For a change, Prithvi decided to board the bus from our bus stop. It was either because he wanted to motivate us, or he was completely fond of his new friend circle by now.

'Ready to set high scores this time too?' asked Aradhna Di, peeping into his revision.

'I will try this time,' said Prithvi. He looked at all of us and said, 'looks like I've got tough competition this time.'

It was hard to say if he actually meant that, but for us it was a compliment. A few minutes before the bus was due to arrive, Prithvi called me to one side and asked, 'How is Tamanna after that chain snatching incident? I am sorry, I completely forgot about it.'

'Well, that's okay,' I said. 'She seems to be fine. Avni told Aradhna Di that the incident happened inside our area and not in CP. She panicked for some time but relaxed later.'

'What about Aarav?'

'He surprised me,' I said and described the caring nature he had displayed that day.

'I had some doubt in my mind when I first interacted with you all in the school. I got some smell of uneasiness between them.'

'But he is again ignoring her today,' I said, watching Aarav, who was busy revising his notes. His mood kept changing like the weather. I didn't know what thoughts were running in his mind that he was completely unaware or trying to be unaware of a girl who loved him so much.

'You are seeing only what you want to see,' said Prithvi. 'Just look now.'

When I looked towards Aarav again, I was happy to see that he was trying to catch a glimpse of Tamanna secretively, without being noticed. It was hard for me to believe that; whatever Prithvi did or showed was hard for me to believe. Soon, we heard the sound of our bus and I realized that I would get only a few more minutes for revision before I reached school.

I was sitting in the examination hall, one hour had already passed and still long lists of questions remained in front of me. My mind was still stuck with what Prithvi had said - you are seeing only what you want to see. And, I could not help but relate it to Iqbal. The previous night when I had met him, he asked me, 'do you have any idea where I come from?'

It was midnight. The cold and the tone by which he spoke to me was harsh. I suddenly turned back after feeling someone's presence at the end of the narrow lane where we were standing. For the first time, I felt that Iqbal was not alone. It might be due to my overthinking that I sensed eerie shadows creeping across the walls under the streetlights.

'I assume that you heard me,' said Iqbal, reminding me that I had to answer his question.

'No...I mean...I-I don't have the answer to your question.'

'I'll not lie to you,' said Iqbal, keeping his hand on top of my head. 'The right time will come when you'll know everything about me. All I could say now is that I've come from a place far away from here. It's sometimes difficult to talk about one's own origin.'

Why would he say something like that? Doesn't he belong to the Indian soil? I thought still looking at the questions in front of me. Controlling my thoughts, I resumed my writing as I wanted to finish my paper in time. When you know everything, you pray that time should pass slowly and when you are blank, you wonder why the hell your watch is slow! As I was writing, I heard some murmurs around me. When I looked to my side, it was Nikhil who was demonstrating how to hold the answer sheet so that he could view the content easily. His act reminded me of my old days, before the principal confronted me, when I use to throw paper bits to call that person who had studied everything.

'Nikhil, do you want to go out?' asked the invigilator, who stopped him and looked at him as if he was a pickpocket. Two hours passed and now it was just a half-hour play. I had taken only one supplementary sheet while others had two or three in their stock. It was quite irritating and frustrating when your fellow students took more supplementary sheets than you.

Soon, I heard the final bell and saw the invigilator collecting the answer sheets in a hurry as if he was on a hunting mission. I handed over my paper and came out of the hall along with Prithvi and Youhaan. We discussed about the paper, clarifying our doubts. The result of the discussion was that our paper was good, and we could expect good marks in our first subject. When your first exam goes well, it is really a confidence booster for the forthcoming ones. I gave a satisfactory performance in my other exams—English was awesome, Mathematics was a little tough but enough to pass, Hindi was again good, and lastly, there was Chemistry, which was the toughest, but I was sure that I could get passing marks. But there was one subject whose syllabus was getting tougher day by day.

'Do you have a plan for me?' asked Iqbal, calling me again for a discussion one night. He was really getting on my nerves due to his constant demand to meet us.

'I am getting there slowly,' I said, giving him an assurance. 'We're waiting for a Sunday to complete your last job.'

'Good,' he said. 'I presume you're trying to get rid of me now.'

It was somewhat true. I could neither deny it, nor could I give him a false consolation. Choosing a safe way in between those two options was the best solution for me. 'All we want is to complete what we had started,' I said.

'I have my eyes on you,' said Iqbal this time giving me a verbal warning. As the days passed, the first impression that he had on me was slowly fading away. He was turning into someone whom I was totally unaware of. What Prithvi said might be true, I thought.

'You must also tell me about those locations now where you kept my weapons,' said Iqbal.

'Alright, it goes like this,' I said and one by one I narrated each location to him properly.

'I must say you did a good job, see you,' he said, feeling satisfied with my answer.

He disappeared again in the dark leaving me in a baffled state. I felt like being the centre of a rope in the game of tug of war. One side of the rope was pulled by Iqbal and the other by Prithvi. Where one offered a chance to revive from the ashes of indignity the other always preached the virtue of goodness. It was difficult to tell who pulled the rope stronger, but I felt the momentum going towards

Prithvi. That day was also important because Iqbal never asked to meet me after that. I don't know what happened. It was better to conclude by saying that the darkness had swallowed him.

The Adolescent Years

It was mid-February, but it seemed there was no end to the cold, it was still ferocious with its sharp teeth. Our pre-Board results were declared a week ago. We had all passed with good marks and even our principal couldn't believe how we did it. Why blame the principal? Even we couldn't believe how we did it!

Looking at our marks, we were confident that we could do better in our Boards. Di was so happy that she distributed sweets in her office. All these changes in our approach towards exams was because of Prithvi, our miracle man. He made the last year of our school memorable and its every moment got imprinted in our senses. And now, it was time to take care and preserve those moments carefully in our hearts, as it was our farewell day.

It was 8:30 am when we called up Prithvi and asked him to come up to our home so that we could all leave together for school, for our farewell function.

'Dad...Mom, I am leaving, will return in the evening,' said Prithvi, as he took his bag and was about to leave for our home.

'Your farewell function is from 2:00 pm, right?' asked his dad, folding the newspaper which he was reading. 'Why are you leaving now?'

'I'll go with Samarth and group, I am going to their house.'

'Okay, but go safely,' said his mom from the kitchen where she was kneading the dough for breakfast.

'Don't worry mom, your son will be fine.'

'Yes, my son will be fine; he knows to take care of himself,' supported his dad.

'Dad, you rock.'

'I know you and your dad are on one side,' said his mom as she kept on kneading until the dough was smooth and no longer sticky.

'I love you, mom,' said Prithvi, giving a flying kiss and he opened the door.

He always liked to take a walk to his destination if it was only a short distance ahead, enjoying the sight of people walking around, looking at their activities, greeting people he knew, and admiring the surroundings. That day also, he followed his habit and took a short walk to our home. But before coming to our home, he headed towards Radhika's house. Though he never said it to me or anyone else, I knew that he loved her very much. They had been friends from the past eight years and all these years, Radhika had shown good signs of improvement. Thanks to her friendship with Prithvi, she had taken a long leap from her dark life to a brighter one. She took a little longer time to learn language, develop social skills and take care of her personal needs, such as dressing or eating. Her family, of course, helped her but it was Prithvi who always stood with her as a support. He tried his level best to develop her potential to the fullest.

'Hi, Prithvi,' greeted Meera, opening the door for him.

'Hi, you wanted to go to Avni's house, let's go.'

'I've some work now,' said Meera, scratching the back of head. 'Do one thing, you take Radhika along with you. I'll be there in an hour.'

'Alright.'

'Here she comes,' said Meera, gesturing towards Radhika, who came and stood alongside her wearing a beautiful dress and covering herself with a brown shawl. She was looking divine in that outfit and Prithvi was mesmerized seeing her.

'Shall we go?' he asked and Radhika simply nodded her head. Prithvi adjusted her shawl and said, 'Now, it's perfect.'

They started walking like a new couple who were going on a date for the first time. Radhika was a little shy most of the time, gazing down at the road while Prithvi, who was quite cool, admired her continuously.

'Would you mind walking a little closer?' he asked and Radhika slowly moved towards him. 'Are you fine?' he enquired, feeling that something was troubling her. Radhika gave her answer by just looking into his eyes, a look that portrayed love. Everything was fine in those gentle eyes.

If you imagine the world as a forest, these two would be the butterflies flying among the tall trees and dense bushes. However deep the forest may be or messy the tangled roots, nothing could obscure their way. They would come out flying into the open air and under the pure light of the day. They were blessed with an unbounded capacity that no obstruction had the power to stop them.

'Have you ever been to Paranthewali Gali?' asked Prithvi, generating curiosity in her.

'No,' said Radhika, moving her head.

'It's in our locality and is very popular,' said Prithvi with enthusiasm. 'I've heard that in UK and in Bombay, restaurant groups are trying to copy the ambience of this famous Old Delhi lane. Would you like to come with me?'

Radhika was reluctant in agreeing. Prithvi could read her mind and said, 'I know you want to spend some time with me, so I am making it easy for us.'

She again gave her approval through her eyes, eyes that portrayed affection.

Paranthewali Gali is the name of a narrow street in the Chandni Chowk area of Old Delhi, noted for its *parantha* makers who had been running their shops for at least six generations.

'*Bhaiya ji*, two *matar paranthas*, quickly,' said Prithvi, giving the order. He came and placed himself alongside Radhika and said, 'I read somewhere that years just after Independence, Jawaharlal Nehru, Indira Gandhi, and Vijayalakshmi Pandit came to savour *parantha* meals in this *gali*.'

'I thought you were about to get a little romantic,' said Radhika, surprising him.

'You know, some habits don't change,' said Prithvi laughingly. 'Here comes the food.'

His order was soon ready and was served on the table—*matar parantha* with sweet tamarind chutney, mixed vegetable pickle and potato curry. In short, it was a mouth-watering dish.

'I want to taste the food from your hand, as I always do,' said Radhika.

'How do you feel when you are with me?' asked Prithvi, putting a piece of *parantha* into Radhika's mouth.

'I feel the same way you feel.'

'I always feel like I am hearing pianos being played, even in this noisy crowd.'

Radhika was not in a mood to understand the meaning of those fancy lines. Firstly, it didn't suit Prithvi's image, and secondly, she preferred a simpler way of expression. For her, the virtue in simplicity was preferable to exaggeration.

'I know you want romance in a simpler way, right?' asked Prithvi, understanding her silence. 'Anyways, how is the food?'

'It's really nice,' said Radhika. She was absolutely enjoying the tasty delicacies.

'I've tasted it many times but today, the taste is at its best; I think it's because of you.'

Radhika was happy to hear that. Prithvi always made sure that she got to play the important part in all the aspects that concerned him. Maybe that was the reason Radhika enjoyed his company. She was the first in everything.

Love is like an unexpected snowfall; when you think the winter will be over soon, snow comes in as a surprise. Similarly, when you think life is well settled, love knocks at the door. The same was happening with Prithvi and Radhika; love had already knocked and got in.

'I think we should move, it's getting late,' said Radhika.

'I wish time moved a little slower,' said Prithvi, with a cute expression of dissatisfaction. He got up, paid the bill and they resumed their romantic walk again. They walked, walked and walked and finally stood in between the two three-storied buildings, their destination.

'You go upstairs; your friends must be waiting for you. I'll see you in the evening,' said Prithvi.

'Evening? That's too long.'

'I know...especially for me when I want to give you a surprise.'

Radhika was excited on hearing that. She couldn't wait until the evening and she started urging him to reveal the surprise.

'Surprises are given at the decided time,' said Prithvi, calming her down.

'Can I get a hint at least, please?'

'Alright, I can give you a hint,' said Prithvi and he slowly moved towards her. Radhika's happy smile became a nervous smile. She moved a few steps back but stopped at one point. He looked at her for a minute continuously without blinking and so did she. He brought his lips closer to her ear and whispered two words - *Ana Behibek.*

'What?'

'You'll soon come to know,' said Prithvi touching her nose with his finger. 'Today evening, you'll hear what you waited to hear. Meet me near that flower shop you always visit near your home.'

Radhika turned away smiling and then started climbing the staircase, bidding goodbye to Prithvi. Like the white feathers that float calmly in the thin air, Prithvi's soft voice would always linger within her.

I was in my room and was busy ironing my shirt for the function when I heard the doorbell ringing. I came out of my room and saw Prithvi being welcomed by Di.

'I was waiting for you, come,' I said.

'You get in, I'll bring tea for you,' said Di and she went into the kitchen.

'Don't you think you took too long to reach here?'

'Yes, I was with Radhika actually; I dropped her to the front building.'

'I guessed it right. Let me ask you something...you love her?' I asked as he entered the room. By now I had established such a good rapport with him that I could ask questions related to his personal life.

'Some relationships can never be explained, they just become our habit.'

'You answered my question indirectly. Then say it to her.'

'I'll...let the sunset come.'

'Oh my God, I am damn excited,' I said, jumping on my bed. 'Well, in that case I've a gift for you.'

'Wow, what?'

'Here it is,' said Di suddenly from behind. She was standing with the gift box in her hand accompanied by Aarav, Mihir and Youhaan.

'For you, with love, from all of us,' she said, handing the gift to him.

Prithvi smiled and opened it with utmost curiosity. Inside it was a beautiful, white-coloured shirt.

'This is awesome, I love it. I am going to wear this for the farewell,' said Prithvi with a big smile on his face. As he said farewell, I again got emotional, remembering some happy memories of my school life. I remembered how I was when I newly joined the school and what I had become at the time of passing out. In those few minutes, I took a trip down memory lane, a 14-year-long trip.

The stage set up, teachers and staff members dressed so well, the atmosphere around me, and the cold waves all took me back to the day of the annual function. My farewell function was not organized at the same budget level of the annual function, but it did not lack in anything.

We all were sitting together somewhere in the middle. We enjoyed the programme a lot. I had never imagined that I'd enjoy my farewell with Prithvi. The programme started with God's blessings, followed by a prayer song. The anchors called out the names of all the students who belonged to the outgoing batch. When my name was called, I felt like crying, the reason being it was the last time my name would be echoed in this campus. As per the order of the names called, one by one, everyone went on to the stage to give their respective introductions. The toughest job for me was to face those friendly questions asked by our principal and teachers. The introduction rounds were organized at regular breaks and those breaks had the real charm of the function, with all the best dances, singing, skits and more.

The function continued with a few emotional songs. We enjoyed some good dance performances. There were three game shows that were organized for us, one being a quiz show and the other one, a vocabulary game where one had to translate the respective English words into pure Hindi. The last show was the sari-wearing competition. We laughed out loud when Mihir's name was called for the sari-wearing competition in a random pick and we laughed to death when he won it. He proved that he could be a beautiful woman too. Every programme item was welcomed by loud shouts and huge applause. Everyone was enjoying the event to their fullest, knowing this was the last school function they were attending. For the first time in my life, I saw Avni in a saree. She was looking lovely, delightful and glamorous.

My school was the only place where I was able to see my love, Avni. After getting out from here, I would again have to live that hide-and-seek life. The same conditions applied to my brothers, excluding Aarav, because he still continued to play with his own emotions.

'Guys, tell me what we have for food?' asked Mihir, breaking up the laughter-filled atmosphere around him.

I was about to answer him when our principal came on the stage to give his blessings to the outgoing batch and to wish us good luck. He talked for a little while, but I only remember his last few lines because it got us really excited. He was about to announce the Student of the Year award. We all knew the name but were waiting for it to come out of his mouth.

'Finally, another academic session is at its climax and we've another outgoing batch in front of us,' he said.

'Putting a full stop to my words, I just wish that may all your creations, thinking, dreams and imaginations get the wings you desire. We again have a Student of the Year award. This time, the Student of the Year award goes to none other than our meritorious student, Prithvi!' he said.

As soon as he completed his sentence, we all stood up and started clapping and shouting. We pushed Prithvi to go quickly and he reached the stage running. He reached near the principal and respectfully took his trophy. Our principal hugged him and asked him to say a few words.

'I never expected this award,' he said, holding the mic. 'But I am happy that I received another great appreciation from my school before I pass out. I am humbled and emotional. This school has been my life, and it has my soul. Years after, when I'll travel through these familiar roads, I'll remember that moment when I used to dedicate myself to my books. I'll remember the classroom inside which the words written on the blackboard were my only friends. I'll remember all those instances that taught me how to dream. When I step into the outer world, I'll definitely miss those corridors where I had spent my lonely times. My teachers... I'll definitely miss them and their scolding. I wasn't that lucky when it came to making friends but yes, this last year has gifted me some amazing friends for a lifetime—in short, a new family. This award is incomplete without them; I request all of you to come onstage.'

Avni became emotional when she heard him speaking. I consoled her and we all started to move to the stage. We reached onstage and stood around Prithvi.

'During the past one-and-a-half years,' continued Prithvi. 'I was busy making a song and the good news is,

I've completed it. I would like to sing it for my friends, for my teachers, for my principal, and of course for this heaven—my school.'

He borrowed a guitar from the band group and started singing his self-composed song. It was that same song which I had heard a lot of times whenever he was around me. I'd heard him singing the same song during the annual day auditions, at Aradhna Di's house and now here. But this time, it was quite emotional and special. He completed half of the song and we all hugged him, it was a group hug. We all squeezed him almost, but he didn't yell out; rather, he was laughing and looking towards the fading evening sky above.

By the end, I made an album in my heart. An album made by the memories of yesteryears. Inside it were white pages depicting my 14-year long journey, with photographs of unforgettable moments from the past.

The Guilt Feeling

The farewell function ended with a dinner where students and teachers shared their precious and unforgettable memories. After the dinner, we had a photography session where we posed in different styles and at different places all over the school. We made good use of our new mobile, clicking many pictures that would be viewed and saved by us for the coming years of our life. Youhaan was with his camera, clicking perfect pictures in his own professional style.

'Hey! Don't take everybody to those locations where we have hidden those bags,' said Mihir, in between those sessions.

'Relax,' I said.

Anjali Ma'am was quite emotional and effusive because after our passing out, she would have to make new friends. We assured her that we would be in touch with her always.

'I'll miss you all a lot,' said Ma'am.

'We will miss you too,' I said.

When I grow up and remember these moments, there will be a smile on my lips, a tear waiting to fall from my eyes, and the moments of this day in my heart. With that, the nostalgic evening ended. We all started moving in our own directions with an outpouring of emotions in our heart, with the unrestrained effect of the evening, and with warm-hearted wishes for each other's coming future.

The colourful present of those days would soon become the black and white past of the days to come. We all reached in front of the gate when Prithvi turned back and said, 'Hasta la vista,' looking at the school.

It was around 6:30 pm in the evening when we reached home. As soon as we entered, Di was very happy to see us. We shared with her every exciting thing that happened in the function.

'Di, can I use your kitchen?' asked Prithvi suddenly, interrupting our conversation.

'If you want anything, just tell me; I'll get it for you,' said Di.

'I drink coffee when I am too happy, would you mind a cup with me?'

'Di, he makes the world's best coffee, believe me,' said Mihir, remembering the last time he had tasted his coffee. Mihir's confidence persuaded Di to give it a try.

'Then I don't mind a cup,' she replied smilingly.

Prithvi entered the kitchen and within 10 minutes, he was ready with his coffee. He entered the hall with the tray of coffee cups and served us all one by one, exactly like he did in his home.

'Hey, can I use your phone for a minute?' he asked, serving the coffee to me.

'Of course,' I said, handing the phone to him. I held his hands to give him an important message before he left. 'Be careful about the phone. Di doesn't know about it.'

'Don't worry,' he said and entered Di's room slowly. He saw she was busy arranging the clothes into the cupboard.

'Coffee is ready,' he said.

'Well then, I must taste it,' said Di, taking the cup and having a sip. Impressed by the rich, strong flavour of the brewed coffee she said, 'It's awesome, Mihir was right.'

'Thank you,' said Prithvi, expressing his gratitude. 'I wanted to ask you something.' Prithvi kept the tray on the table and gently rubbed his forehead in nervousness. He was about to ask something about which he himself was unsure. He didn't know what its outcome would be.

'For how long this will continue?' he said, keeping the phone inside his pocket. 'All eight of you walk in opposite directions after standing between these two buildings. These buildings are divided by just a street in between, not by the unwanted problems you all have.'

'I think we should not talk about this,' said Di, feeling irritated at how a 17-year-old boy could question an age-old family problem between two sisters. Prithvi, being a young boy, was not supposed to cross certain boundaries of an adult's personal life. The effect of this disobedience was visible on Aastha Di's face. She was agitated.

'We should talk, because this is about the existence of your family,' continued Prithvi. 'We all don't know how long we are going to live, but till that day, we need to live together.'

'It's not that I don't consider all these things; it's her, she is the one who doesn't care at all.'

'Maybe, she needs a little support from you to understand.'

'You are taking her side?'

'No, I am taking neither your side nor hers. I am taking the side of my friends; they all know each other from their childhood. They all deserve to live freely and express their friendship.'

'What you want me to do?'

'I want you both to patch up.'

'There is no objection from my side, but considering Aradhna, it is not possible in this life.'

'Can you tell me the reason? If you think I am your family.'

She was quiet for some time. Prithvi understood that she wasn't keen on discussing this matter anymore and he started turning back. He thought it was better to step back rather than making the situation worse.

'Wait,' said Di, stopping him. She walked towards him and said, 'It was during the years of our graduation, when our parents died in a road accident.'

Aastha Di began to narrate events that she had never shared with us. She continued, 'I forced my parents to go out that day. If I had not forced them, they would have been alive even today. I didn't know that I was committing the biggest mistake of my life. Years later, I shared this incident with Aradhna and...' said Di. Her eyes were now wet, and she was close to breaking down.

'But why did you force them to go out?'

'It was Aradhna's birthday. I had planned a surprise for her that day and I sent my parents to buy the best gift for her available in the city. But they returned with the biggest shock of our lives—they returned as lifeless corpses.'

'You could have told her this before,' said Prithvi placing his hands around her shoulders and consoling her. Aastha Di was now in tears.

'I tried to tell her everything,' she said, 'but she was not in a state of mind to hear the complete truth. We had a serious conversation following this and she broke all ties with me. I tried hard to make her understand, but I failed.'

'Don't worry Di, she will understand that what happened was just fate.'

'She will never listen to me.'

'She is listening to you.'

'What do you mean?' asked Di, wiping off her tears. Prithvi took out the mobile phone from his pocket in front of her. She was confused for a moment but in a few seconds, she understood everything.

'You called her?' asked Di. As soon as she said this, she heard someone talking on the phone. The call was still on and the person on the other side was none other than Aradhna Di.

'Hello...Di,' came the faint voice from the phone.

'Before entering the room, I had dialled her number and kept the call on. She is hearing you still, talk,' said Prithvi, handing over the phone to her.

Hello...

Di, it's me, I've heard everything.

Whomsoever I've met in my life, no one believed me when I told them about what happened in that room that day. They thought I was coming straight after reading a fantasy novel, or I was highly influenced by some unrealistic dramas. I couldn't make them understand that sometimes things happen beyond logic and reasoning. Setting aside our self-centred nature, we should be liberal enough to accept them.

We were watching TV when we heard the sound of the doorbell. Mihir opened the door and seeing Aradhna Di in front of him, he almost fainted. Aarav, Youhaan and I stood up, not even realizing what we were doing and looked at each other as if we'd got a high voltage shock. She was in tears and straightaway ran into Di's room.

We followed her without even thinking. Aastha Di stood up after seeing her. They both were in tears. Both had care in each other's eyes once again, both once again had love for each other. They came close and continued to look at each other for a minute. For the first time, after these many years, they had made eye contact. They were exchanging their deep, hidden love with all their tears. They hugged tightly, like they used to do in their childhood when they were very happy, not allowing any force to separate them. The old sisters were back.

'Di, you are here?' asked Sandhya who came in suddenly. She was equally spellbound like us by the scene and so were the other three girls who followed.

'Won't you guys celebrate this?' asked Prithvi to all of us.

Celebration seemed to be a far-fetched thing when we still couldn't digest the truth in front of us.

'C'mon guys, just hug them tightly,' said Prithvi, encouraging us again. We ran with full enthusiasm towards them and gave them a tight, long hug. It was the most wonderful moment of my life. Though Prithvi was not singing, I could hear his song playing in the background. I definitely knew it had happened because of him. I was waiting for the biggest miracle and it was here with me. This biggest miracle of his was surely the happiest of all.

'Can I have a family photo?' asked Prithvi who kept the mobile on the table and set it on timer. He came running towards us, saying 'cheese' and the photograph was clicked, making the picture-perfect family again.

It was 7:00 pm and we all were sitting in the hall, talking to each other. After years, we were talking to the girls in our own home. Both the big sisters were busy in the kitchen and I was sure they both were still crying.

'Well, I need to go, it's late now,' said Prithvi, getting up.

As he was going downstairs, I stopped him and asked, 'You are going for Radhika, right?'

'Smart boy,' he replied, winking at me. 'I am taking your phone for today. I need to inform Dad that I'll be late. And don't worry, I told Di that this is my phone.'

'Of course, I know you must have handled that. Just make this day worth remembering for Radhika, like you did for us.'

'Don't worry, I love gifting happiness to others,' said Prithvi and he was off. I rushed up, gathered all my family members and reached the terrace. I looked down and saw Prithvi walking out. I shouted, '*Prrithviiiii...!*'

He looked upwards and we all waved goodbye. He waved back at us smilingly, giving assurance that he would continue to meet us like this and give us surprises.

The farewell day was over, and it was another morning for all of us. But that morning was not at all ordinary for us. Both the big sisters were sleeping in one room after many years. We vacated our room for the girls, and we four boys slept in the hall. It was the best morning I'd witnessed in my life after these many years. Suddenly I heard the phone ringing. Only I was awake then, so without disturbing the others, I stood up to attend the phone. I thought it was Prithvi, he must be calling for sharing the experiences of his confession night.

Hello, I said.

Hello...Samarth?

Yes.

Samarth, this is Meera...

My hands were fumbling and trembling while I was holding the phone receiver. I felt as if the world before me was spinning too fast. I was no less than a dead body. I sat on my knees, and my eyes were almost filled to the brim, ready to burst out. I remembered the words spoken by Prithvi to Aarav...' there will be a day, the day when I'll give you a big shock. The shock will make you go bewildered.' He had never talked about any revenge, but I never imagined that God would make his words come true in this manner.

A tear rolled down from my eye as I remembered that line. I came to know what the feeling of guilt was. Crying like a mad man, I closed my ears as those words from Meera echoed around me. Hearing me cry, the others woke up. Youhaan asked me what happened. 'Why are you crying?' Hearing his shout, everyone else came out running too. Di turned my crying face towards her and asked, 'Samarth, what happened, why are you crying?'

I couldn't utter a single word, my throat was dry due to the shock, I didn't know how to tell them all that the reason for their togetherness was now no more.

'Please, tell us. What happened?' said Aradhna Di.

'Prithvi is no more Di...he is no more,' I said it finally.

Di hugged me tightly as soon as she heard it. There was complete silence around me; I could only hear the sounds of my own sobs. After some time, I felt tears pouring from Di's eyes—she was still hugging me. Nobody could believe that what I said was true, especially Mihir and Youhaan who were saying frustratedly that I was insane. Sandhya and Suhaani were crying and hugging Aradhna Di, who was also sitting like a paralyzed person who only knows how to shed tears. Avni and Tamanna were sitting near me, but they also didn't believe me and were looking at the others crying, as if they didn't know what had happened.

I saw the door open and understood that Aarav must be on the terrace. Tamanna went to the terrace and saw Aarav crying and yelling. She straightaway went towards him and hugged him. This time he didn't ignore her, the love living in his heart had come out into existence. They were supporting each other and consoling each other that the truth has to be accepted. Prithvi must have been seeing them both from the skies and would be feeling very happy to see the real Aarav.

We were standing at the cremation ground, where, in front of my eyes, lay a burning Prithvi. The miracle man, with all his miracles, was slowly turning into ashes. We visualised his dead body lying on one of the streets of Chandni Chowk, the white shirt we had gifted him on the farewell day now stained with blood. The reason for his death was still a mystery. We were not even allowed to touch his body because the police had made it a murder case and their investigation was on. We all wanted to forget that scene where we saw our friend killed so mercilessly. His parents were shattered, having lost their beloved son. The most heart-breaking scene for me was to see Radhika standing like a corpse along with her sister. It would have been easier for me to see her crying but not standing like a lifeless person.

Meera knew the place where Radhika was supposed to meet Prithvi. She told me that when she went there, she found a lifeless Prithvi. Meera also found Radhika in an unconscious state at a certain distance. That disturbing image of Prithvi had made her go weak. That particular scene disturbed her mental balance; she did not believe anyone who said that he was dead. She didn't believe it even after seeing him stained in blood. If his death was a shock for us, it would have been a thunderstorm for Radhika. Her biggest support, her special friend, and of course, the love of her life now lived only in remembrance.

Prithvi and all the memories of him were now playing in front of me. When we were kids, Di used to tell us stories about angels, how they enter into the lives of the ordinary people like a ray of hope, how they make everything alright, and how they ultimately disappear, leaving no trace. Prithvi was neither the villain nor the hero of my story. He was the angel who opened the right doors for us. I wished to see him among the doves that fly in the daylight, in the setting rays of the evening sun, and in my dreams where he'd wish me goodnight.

There's a belief that humans are born again and again according to their karma, until they finally gain liberation from rebirth—moksha. By living a life of value without sin, it is possible to come closer to moksha, and perhaps be reborn in a higher form in the next life. I really hoped it should be true, because I wanted to be born as Prithvi's friend again and this time, even closer to him than I had been.

Inferno

Two days passed and things were not as they were before. I could not have thought that things would change so drastically, and that too with such speed. Though both the sisters were at ease with each other now, they still decided to live separately. We boys and girls had grown up now; soon, we were going to be adults and required our own, private spaces. Keeping that in mind, we decided to continue living as we did earlier, but there was no more hatred, only love.

I thought my life had gone back two years; all the same happiness that prevailed at that time was coming back to me. But I was not in a mood to celebrate this; neither was anyone else, because this happiness was incomplete without Prithvi. Our principal declared school closed for one day as a condolence for his death. Our school had lost a real gem. We only hoped that his soul still resided somewhere around us and would be happy seeing all of us back together.

I had a deep amount of sorrow for the death of my special friend, but at the same time I had a feeling of revenge. Revenge for the person who killed him, revenge for the person who committed the biggest sin of his life, and revenge for the person who destroyed our paradise.

Police were still continuing their investigation; we regularly visited almost all news channels to get the latest update of the case. Prithvi's photo was found in newspapers every day, but the identity of his murderer was still under cover. Investigators were still around looking for eyewitnesses but failed to find any. They questioned Meera about that night, and she told them everything that she knew. They traced one or two people who had the courage to speak up. These individuals informed the investigators that they had seen a group of masked men chasing a boy and then finally, shooting him to death. The fact that the murderers were still roaming around the streets freely made my blood boil, but when I saw my united family around me, I just cooled down.

Sadness was definitely visible in all our faces, but we pretended to smile to become each other's moral support. When members of a family become your moral support, you slowly learn to drive away the negativity around you. I was preparing myself to learn all that, but you don't know when the black shadows will again knock on your door.

'Someone please open the door, can't you hear the knocking of the door!' shouted Aradhna Di from the kitchen. Only Aarav, she and I were present at home. The rest were headed to my school as it was the parent-teacher meet, the day when our pre-Board results were officially displayed to our parents. I opted for not going as my mind was disturbed. Aarav and Aradhna Di supported me by staying back. I came back from my thoughts to the present and opened the door. There were two persons standing there but they were not ordinary people. They were policemen.

'I am Kishen Singh; I believe we have met before.'

'Please come in sir,' I said and called Di.

Within no time, Aarav and Di were with me and were staring at the two police officers who were sitting in front of us.

'Is there any problem, sir?' asked Di.

'Well, there is,' said the inspector in a serious tone. 'We've come here to know about Prithvi. What was your relationship with him?'

'He was our friend, sir, and a very special one indeed,' said Aarav.

'Yes sir, he was close to all of us,' said Di.

'Okay, I want to show something to you all. Have a look at this.'

He took out a mobile phone from his pocket and displayed it to us. In that moment, I was really taken aback because the phone was none other than ours. We had given it to Prithvi on the farewell day and I had completely forgotten about it afterwards. Kishen Sir stood up and showed a few photos taken with the phone camera to Di and us. There were photos of our school farewell function and a few family pictures. The last picture clicked by Prithvi was the one when my entire family reunited.

'I believe this is Prithvi's mobile?' Di asked us.

We were speechless. We could not admit the truth as no one knew we had bought it. Even if we found the courage to confess, we had no answer as to where we got the money.

'If it is his phone, then he must be definitely involved in some criminal activities,' said the inspector.

'No sir, he was not that kind of a person,' I objected.

'What do you mean, Inspector?' asked Di.

'I mean this,' he said, and he again showed us a few pictures, handing over the mobile to me. But the pictures we saw this time were shocking. Those pictures were never clicked by us, but they were there in my phone. The pictures showed a group of men handling arms and ammunitions and some of them working on some electric circuitry. We had no idea how these photos were clicked on our phone.

'We were going through his phone when we got these pictures. It seems the area is somewhere around here, and this guy is definitely involved in all these activities,' said the inspector.

I thought then that it was time to admit the truth because I could listen to everything but not false allegations about Prithvi.

'He is innocent sir,' I said, all of a sudden.

'How can you say that?'

'Because the phone is ours. He took it from us two days before he died because he needed to call his dad and inform him about his returning home late,' I said.

Aarav placed his hand on my shoulders, signalling me to slow down and stop admitting everything.

'What? You have a phone? Does Di know about this?' asked Aradhna Di.

I was silent to that question and my silence answered everything, leaving Di in shock.

'This is your phone and your family members don't know anything about it?' enquired the inspector. I was again silent and so was Aarav.

'I think further interrogation should be in the police station,' he said, giving us a severe bout of jitters. 'Get ready, we need to go now.'

That moment, we shrivelled up inside, sweating from top to bottom. You may have big fears in your life, you may have scary phobias in your life, but nothing compares to what you feel when a police officer says to you... *you need to come to the station.*

'You cannot take them like that,' said Di.

'We are just doing our duty ma'am, please co-operate.'

We were ready to walk down but I only regretted one thing—the shame and embarrassment that would be imprinted on my family's face when Aarav and I would get into the police vehicle. We walked out of the door but then suddenly, Kishen Sir's phone began to ring. He took the call, but in seconds, he yelled, '*Whhaaaatt?*'

We wondered why he yelled out so loud. I thought maybe the culprit behind Prithvi's murder was under arrest, but it was something else, something I'd never dreamt of.

'Please switch on the news channel,' he said in a hurried, frightened voice. Di quickly switched on the TV and pressed one of the regularly viewed news channels. We all stood electrified on seeing the clippings. I was scared as hell and felt as if I was having an encounter with some ghost. The clippings telecast a shopping mall near our school with the 'Breaking News' caption blinking again and again at the top of the screen. The clippings also had a caption below, saying 'Under Attack'.

It's doomsday for the NewGen Shopping Mall as it's under a terrorist attack. The terrorists have captured a bus full of passengers that was headed towards a school located nearby. The passengers are now hostages inside this shopping mall. A large number of parents and students are trapped inside, along with a few citizens who were here for shopping. Police has cordoned off the area from all four corners, and we can still hear the sound of firing from inside.

Every word the news reporter spelled out was like thorns penetrating into the flesh of our hearts. Di was on her knees and she started breathing heavily. Meanwhile, on the TV, a few witnesses who saw the whole incident and informed the police had many things to say:

We saw them coming with full force with their faces covered. They had big guns with them and with those, they forced the driver to stop the bus.

They got hold of every passenger on the bus, not leaving a single one. The driver was forced to change the route of the bus and they headed towards the shopping mall.

An anonymous bystander had made a minute-long clip on his mobile phone of the whole incident and the channel was broadcasting the same. We saw the clip and it was terror at its extreme. We saw the crowd shouting, the sound of life-taking guns and a somewhat blurred image of a woman. I knew her well—she was none other than my Aastha Di. It was easy for me to imagine who the others would be. I felt like I was dead.

'Samarth, call Di,' said Aradhna Di to me.

I quickly dialled her number, but it was out of coverage area. I slammed the receiver hard out of anger and frustration, not knowing what to do. We were assured of one thing—that excluding us three, all my family was inside the mall. *What would be their condition? Were they safe?* I had no idea. Di kept on changing different channels and all of them had the same thing to say. Di slowly began to cry, and Aarav consoled her saying, 'Nothing will happen Di, they will be alright.'

'We need to go quickly,' said Kishen Sir to his assistant officer standing along his side. They both quickly went out, forgetting that they were about to take us to the station. As soon as they hurried out, I said, 'We need to go quickly to that cursed place.'

Aradhna Di got up, and hurried us downstairs. I placed the mobile back into my pocket and quickly got down. We walked a certain distance to get a taxi. Finally, we got one, but he said, 'Madam, there is a high alert in that area, I can't take a risk.'

'Please *bhai saab*, we have an emergency.'

'Then why should I take the risk, madam?'

'We'll pay you double,' I said.

'If you offer me triple, then also I won't move.'

After many efforts, we were able to persuade the taxi driver. We got in and he accelerated his taxi towards our school area. He dropped us near the mall as he was afraid to take his taxi forward. When we reached the spot, we saw media persons everywhere and a huge crowd of onlookers. Police had cordoned off the area all around, not allowing anyone to come close. We saw that the captured bus was in flames, with black smoke darkening the air above it—and our minds. The area was already declared to be on high alert and the police were continuously in talks with the Defence Ministry. We were worried about Di and the others. I was still unable to understand how all this happened.

Was it the same attack that Iqbal had warned us about? If it was, then we had failed miserably. Even after risking our own lives and making all those efforts, we were unable to prevent this from happening. Failure was not a new thing for us, but this time it cost us badly.

We still don't have any news about the happenings inside the shopping mall and the situation outside here is highly tensed. People are very much worried about their family members and kids while the police are trying their best to take some action.

'Sir, my sister is inside,' said Aradhna Di suddenly, walking to the police camp and crying.

'Madam, please control yourself, we are trying our best,' said an officer.

'Di, come, let them do their duty,' I said and took her aside.

As soon we moved away, we heard the sound of a huge explosion from inside. Fire and fumes were coming out from the first floor of the mall. That was a heart-breaking scene for us. Di was shattered, scared to the extent that she couldn't even scream properly seeing that, and went on her knees. Aarav and I also went down to hold her.

'Nothing will happen to them,' said Aarav.

'Believe in God,' I said. Though I told her to believe in God, I was terribly scared from toe to head. My faith itself was a little low after listening to the people who were being questioned by the reporters.

We were in the ground floor, so luckily and without much difficulty, we came outside alive.

They all were masked and were looking like demons. I don't know in what number they are present inside.

The Premier School, the school nearby, has a parent-teacher meet today. Many of the passengers inside the bus were going for that when suddenly, things changed.

The final verdict of the reporters gave me a clear overview of the situation:

Many parents, along with their kids, are stranded inside and the majority of the people inside are shoppers. Those who were unsuccessful in coming outside are struggling for their existence now. We just really hope that the situation will come under control.

I didn't find Di and the others around me. I didn't find them among the people who had successfully escaped. I couldn't do anything other than to hope for the safety of my family. I just looked around for hands that were offering help, looking for God's grace, a hope for rescue.

Hope Begins

Twenty-four hours passed and we were still waiting outside the shopping mall to hear some positive reports of the situation. It was night-time, and it was cold outside, but we didn't feel any effect of the cold. Our hearts had become cold enough to beat the cold outside.

Police had made the media crew move away to a distance. Within the past few hours, we only witnessed firing sessions in which three police officers were injured severely. But how many casualties had occurred inside, we had no idea. The sound of every gunshot was like lightning striking our ears. Media persons were busy demanding reasons from the government for this security lapse. Many interviews and talk shows were being telecast all over the network. They were continuously updating the situation outside the mall, but there was no one who could offer any positive updates about the situation inside. A few hours later, we heard the sound of a bus coming towards our side. It had a name written on it—NATIONAL SECURITY GUARD.

My eyes widened. Of course, I had heard about the NSG, the elite commando force that has defended the country and saved precious lives and property on memorable occasions in the nation's history. If they were here, clearly, this was something much bigger than what I could imagine.

The bus stopped and a big group of black-suited commandos came out of the door quickly. The last commando to come out was Major Kabir.

'Sir,' saluted Inspector Kishen.

'What is the situation?'

'Very bad, sir.'

'I want the media coverage to be as minimum as possible.'

'Got it, sir.'

'Boys, we need to plan a strategy,' said Major Kabir as he turned away and called his commandos to assemble at one place. They made a circle and the Major took out a blueprint of the shopping mall in front of them. The map displayed the mall with its complete architectural design along with nearby locations. They began to discuss and strategize their plan of action. For the first time in my life, I was seeing the live action of the NSG Black Cats. I'd only heard about them in books, on internet, and on my television set, but never seen them face to face.

'Officer,' called Major Kabir. 'Our map shows that this mall has an adjoining warehouse behind.'

'Yes sir, we have an employee here who can show us the way.'

Di, Aarav, and I were observing the entire happenings from a distance. We hadn't got even a glimpse of our family members since they went out in the morning. We hadn't eaten even a morsel because we felt no hunger in the face of what was happening.

'Come with me,' said Inspector Kishen, pointing towards a man who was dressed in some uniform.

'What happened, sir? Any news about our family?' asked Di, interrupting him.

'I'll tell you soon if we get anything, don't worry,' he said. He again called out to the uniformed man, 'You there, you need to come with me.'

Aarav and I decided to follow him quietly and started walking, wondering why that man was called. We reached near a particular area where we saw Major Kabir standing.

'We need to get to the warehouse,' said Major Kabir. 'You have to show us the way.'

'Y-Yes, sir,' stammered the man. He worked there as an employee of a branded cloth store and was a bundle of nerves.

'Well, we need to get inside as quickly as possible,' said Major Kabir, placing hands on his shoulders. 'Can you please take us there now.'

'Yes sir,' the man replied this time with a little confidence. The bravery in Major Kabir's eyes might have boosted up his morale.

Aarav and I rushed towards the area breaking the security and shouting out:

'*Sir, our family is inside, please save them!*'

'Get back, both of you.'

'Please, listen to me.'

'I said get back! Nothing will happen to anyone as long as we are alive.'

We were pushed hard to a side by the commandos, but we were not ready to give up. We opted for staying there and observing all the proceedings while the policemen were busy controlling the media.

'Ok boys, take your position, we are going inside,' ordered Major Kabir and the commandos geared up to start operations. One by one, they started entering into the warehouse with a bag on their shoulders and their respective guns. Police had forbidden the media to come to the rear side and were stopping them way ahead. The commandos got in successfully and the Major started dividing them into groups.

'Alright guys, this mall has three floors, so we are going to divide ourselves into three groups,' he said in a soft voice. 'Ram, you will lead one. Faiz, you'll lead the second and the rest of you will be under me.'

'Got it, sir.'

'We will attack in different directions; according to the current information, one face of the building is under their custody...so Ram, you reach the top floor, I'll go to the middle and Faiz, you will handle the ground floor. Is that clear?'

'Clear, sir.'

'Then let's get them,' said the Major and they set out in different directions as per the orders.

We were standing outside the warehouse wondering what would be happening inside. I knew that the NSG has maintained an edge over terrorist outfits in possession of latest technology and are considered among the best special operations units in all of Asia. My hope resided with them.

I wished I could have lent my support to them but then, I thought for a moment and said to Aarav meekly in his ears, 'Come, let's get in.'

'Are you mad? We can't.'

'We have to, don't you want your family back safely?'

'I do want that. But the officials here will not allow us.'

'I am not thinking about the officials, I am thinking about Di and others.'

'What about Di then, she will be alone here.'

'Don't worry, she'll be fine,' I said, looking at Aradhna Di.

She was a strong woman. Avni often praised about her inner strength and her ability to withstand deteriorating conditions. 'A woman made this world,' Aradhna Di would say to Avni and the other girls whenever she felt like giving them some valuable guidance. 'When the first woman on earth gave birth to a child, she began a world that grew up this far. We should respect that. The entire human race should respect that. People will definitely doubt our capabilities, but we must make them realize the things that make us stand apart.'

Sacrifice...one among the many things that define the bravery of women and makes them unique. I knew it because I've always seen it. Even that day, though she was scared, Aradhna Di battled her fears with lionhearted efforts. She would be fine even if we were not there.

We started moving towards the warehouse slowly and gently. Kishen Sir was busy on a phone call; maybe he was busy explaining things to his senior officials. We didn't want him to notice us because this was our only chance to do something for our family. Kishen Sir joined his other officers in restricting the media while Di was still standing faraway at the same spot. She didn't move an inch. I could imagine the tears in her eyes. We successfully reached inside without coming under notice. I was quite confident that no one saw us doing this. After getting inside, we sensed the danger lying ahead of us, but we knew that we couldn't back out now.

'Aarav, we will go in different directions, you go to the middle floor and check if anyone is there and the top floor is mine.'

'Sure,' he said, and he hugged me.

'Promise me that you will meet me outside,' I said patting his back.

'I promise,' he said, and he was off.

Di was still outside, addressing the media people making reports and informing the world about the situation there. The whole nation at this time must have been glued to their TV sets waiting to see how the rescue operation would be carried out. The media was somehow prevented from getting any information about the NSG operations that were being conducted. Darkness was slowly fading, and dawn was just about to break on the horizon.

'Madam, you need some water?' asked Kishen Sir, suddenly appearing in front of her.

'No sir,' replied Di, 'I'm fine.'

'Let me ask them,' he said, and he looked around for us. He searched hard but couldn't find us. This made Di more tensed.

'Madam, have you seen them?'

'No.'

'Where are they? They came behind us and we asked them to go back. Did they return?'

He searched here and there but we were missing. He looked towards the warehouse area, stared for a minute and then understood everything. He had a faint memory of us both standing there. He understood why we were missing.

'Oh my God!' he said softly.

The warehouse had a short route to reach to the ground floor. It was used to carry the manufactured goods to the respective stores. The commandos got a hint of this way and decided to make the most of it. Aarav was already on his way while I was slowly gathering all my courage. With each step I took, the sound of the firings was very clear to me. It was an indication that the Black Cats had already begun their job.

I was worried about Aarav. *Will he be okay?* I asked myself. *He'll be definitely okay...*I forced myself to relax. I somehow managed to reach the top floor using the emergency staircase. To be more precise, I was at the entertainment zone, the movie theatre. I took almost an hour to reach there, taking care that I didn't get caught by the commandos who had come to save us or by the other group who were there to slaughter us.

There were four theatres for screening movies and one among them was under a terrifying situation. I could sense it from outside. *It would be foolish to enter directly inside*, I thought, and I decided to enter the projector room. I found a way to reach inside and the scene I saw from there was something I can never forget. I looked through the small square-shaped window from where the film would be projected onto the big screen. A man was walking towards the silver screen with a gun; I could only see his back along with his gun. They had switched on several lights due to which I was able to see quite well. He suddenly turned towards the projector room which forced me to bow down. After a minute, I again peeped through the window and this time, what I saw brought tears to my eyes.

There were many hostages who were saying their prayers. I saw Aastha Di sitting there and looking towards the man with frightened eyes. The man slowly walked towards her, stood in front of her for a minute and then suddenly pointed his gun towards her. She yelled out but her voice didn't have any intensity as she was too stunned. She was not getting her voice to react. I heard the man laughing—it was his trick to scare the hostages more. I had my heart in my mouth when I saw the scene, but I could breathe normally after seeing that she was alright. I searched for the others, but I couldn't see them.

I got into a more comfortable position and then again tried to look for them with the available light. This time I saw them, I saw all of them sitting next to Di with Youhaan and Mihir hugging her tightly. She was astounded and daunted. She was not even looking towards the man and was resting her head against Mihir. At that moment, I was tempted to break in and charge at them. But I made myself relax and tried to think of more practical strategies. I continued watching them and this time I saw Sandhya and Suhaani sitting to the right side of Di and crying continuously while Avni was sitting next to Mihir on his left side. She was shattered and petrified; I knew she needed me the most at that time. I again sunk into dismay seeing her in this dreadful situation.

I saw everyone except Tamanna; she was nowhere to be seen. Suddenly I heard a gunshot from outside and the man inside got alerted. He started firing outside to the commandos. Soon the atmosphere was filled with gunshots and the hostages inside were screaming. I decided to stay in the projector room and hide there till I could find some way to get in. The gunshots continued and I tried to close my ears as tightly as I could, but my mind was open, open to a thought.

Where was Tamanna?

Hard Battle

Tamanna was 10 years old when she was accidentally locked inside a small room in the orphanage. Feeling suffocated and claustrophobic, she cried desperately for help. That time she just had to battle her childish fears of being left alone or dying inside a dusty room. Her fears lasted until Aradhna Di broke the lock and opened the door. It was an act well in time before Tamanna possessed any irrational fear of confined spaces.

But now fears had grown in intensity. The situation was not the same. Tamanna was petrified, much like a duckling who had got detached from her raft. She was sitting inside one of the flower shops in the deserted middle floor of the mall, all alone. There were ghouls outside hungry for her life. There was complete silence inside, and her only company were the dead flowers in that shop. Not a single flower had retained its natural charm or fragrance. They all seemed to be stained by blood. Outside, she could hear the sound of firings, those sounds were bloodcurdling. She was sitting beneath one of the desks in the shop so that no one could see her. The desk was kept at the counter where packing and billing was done. She was even taking her every breath silently.

Aarav was hiding somewhere at the ground floor waiting for a clear scene to move forward. After an hour or so, he slowly got out and was standing on the second flight of stairs waiting for the area to be clear. The Black Cats were battling hard to save the hostages.

'Give me cover fire, I am going ahead,' said Major Kabir.

He went ahead slowly with his gun, with his commandos behind him. He stopped at one point, counted slowly, *one-two-three*, and began to run. He started firing breaking the glass pane of a nearby shop, the shop adjacent to which Tamanna was sitting. The man hiding inside was shot dead; the NSG Black Cats had got their first casualty from the other troop. Tamanna shut her ears tightly on hearing the hair-raising sounds of the firing with such intensity.

'Good work boys,' said the Major. He ordered his commandos to move ahead. They checked the adjacent flower shop and found no one as Tamanna was still keeping quiet and hiding.

'We've an injury on our side sir,' said one of the commandos.

'What happened?'

'Jaswant is hit by a bullet on his shoulder. He was along with Ram Sir at the top floor near the theatre.'

'Is he alright?'

'Fine, sir. We've taken him out.'

'Well, I think there is a huge task to be done at the top floor.'

Aarav slowly moved upwards after sensing that the firing had been stopped for the moment. He reached the end of the stairs to the second floor and slowly peeped to see the situation on the other side. The commandos were moving ahead, and Aarav placed his steps forward without making any sound. He reached the door of one of the shops on the second floor which was near the stairs. He quickly got into the shop and waited for the commandos to clear the area. The shop looked empty, but Aarav could sense an eerie presence of a human inside. He began to walk, and he could clearly hear the sound of his own footsteps. As he moved, he saw someone sitting beneath the desk at the counter. He got alert, thinking it might be someone from the enemy camp. As he moved further ahead, his alertness decreased as he had a feeling that it was someone whom he knew well.

'Who's hiding there?' he asked.

The person slowly raised her head upwards from below the desk; the person looked towards Aarav with her unnerving eyes.

'Tamanna,' spelled Aarav.

Tamanna slowly came out from beneath. She was crying continuously. She stood some distance away from Aarav, looking at him with tearful eyes. After a moment, she ran towards him and hugged him tightly, so tightly that no one could have separated her. Aarav, instead of ignoring her as he always used to, just tightened the hug more. She started crying more and sobbed, 'Don't leave me, please don't leave me.'

Aarav consoled her by hugging her continuously; he was giving her strength to fight the situation, he was easing her, soothing her, and was acting like a tranquilizer.

'Don't worry, I'll not leave you,' he said, while they still hugged.

Outside the mall, Di panicked after knowing that we had gotten inside. She couldn't believe that now her whole family was inside. She was the only one left alone outside.

'Madam, you should have taken care of them,' said Inspector Kishen.

'I am sorry, sir.'

'We are fighting for your safety and then this sort of thing happens.'

'Please don't be harsh on me at this time.'

'Connect me to Major Kabir,' he said to one of the policemen after seeing Di again in tears.

The policeman tried hard to connect to Major, but every time he failed. 'We are not getting through, sir,' said the officer.

'Keep trying,' said Inspector Kishen. 'Don't worry Madam, we will bring your family back,' he said consoling Di.

I was standing inside the washroom and might have spent hours there out of fear. The projector room gave a feel of a slaughterhouse with all the screams of the hostages. The air inside had become breathless and full of fear because of which I came outside. I had closed the door of the washroom from inside so that no one could dash in. Thinking of some way to get into the movie hall, I was running out of ideas. Before the commandos comes to know that two kids had gotten in, I must meet my family.

I slowly opened the door and took a quick look outside. The corridor was clear and diagonally to me, at some distance, was the door to the movie hall. There was no place in this goddam mall where I could go and think of getting my family back safely. I had no choice other than going back to the projector room and find a way this time.

When I was about to enter, I sensed the presence of someone who was already inside before me. *Who could it be?* I managed to peek in. A man was sitting and watching the scene happening down the long row of chairs very attentively, as if he wouldn't like to be disturbed even for a second. But he was disturbed, disturbed by the voice coming in from the Bluetooth device attached to his ear.

Yes?

Situation is bad, we are two down.

Where are you?

Second floor.

I'll be there.

Got it.

He switched off the device and stood up to walk. He turned the other side, but his face was not at all visible in the darkness. He took out a gun from a bag kept on the table. The colour of the bag was quite familiar to me, as if I'd seen it somewhere. Suddenly, he turned towards the door and I bent down quickly. I got a feeling that he had seen me and within no time, I ran out from there.

'How did you come here?' asked Aarav.

He was sitting with Tamanna under the same desk. Tamanna had slowly relaxed in his presence. She was resting her head on his shoulder and he was still providing her strength.

'I don't know when I got detached from Di and the others. I came down running after I lost my way. As soon as I reached down, I heard the sound of the gunshots from the other side. I got scared and I decided to hide here inside.'

'Where are the others?'

'They must be on the top floor.'

'Don't worry, we'll get everybody out of here.'

'I am too scared.'

'Don't need to be scared when I am with you,' said Aarav and he kissed her forehead.

Tamanna looked towards him as she used to look at him always, like a girl who is madly in love with a prince. And for the first time, Aarav reflected his feelings towards her, he was looking at her as if he had never seen her before.

'I always wanted you to be so close to me,' said Tamanna.

'Here I am, fulfilling you wish.'

'How did our world become upside down so quickly? Till yesterday, everything was fine and perfect. We got back our family and today, what's happened?'

'Everything will be fine as before,' said Aarav, bringing some optimism around them. 'We'll come out of this together.'

I ran and reached the middle floor, saving my life. I stopped for just a second to look back and see if the man was following me or not. My fears were true, he was following me, and he was closer. Death - a word that I feared the most in my life was now chasing me in a human form. With all my energy, I ran again and found a place to hide. I suddenly heard a gunshot and saw a bullet bouncing on the floor after striking the wall. The man had fired a blank shot to scare me and he was successful. The word 'death' grew bigger inside my mind.

I waited for the man to reach the opposite side of the place where I was hiding. When he reached the other side, I started running again. He saw me running to the top floor and again pressed the trigger of his gun. Another bullet and I was almost killed. He was about to follow me up, but he was stopped, stopped by hearing a girl's scream. He forgot me completely and started to check from where the scream came.

'Relax, Tamanna, relax, I am still with you,' said Aarav, after Tamanna screamed on hearing the gunshots outside the shop.

'Don't cry, be quiet, we can't take any risk.'

'Please get me out of here, Aarav.'

'Come,' said Aarav and they both stood up to leave.

The man was standing outside the door of the shop and was listening to their conversation. He loaded his gun, opened the door and got in.

The battle was more ferocious and difficult on the top floor. I had only one idea—to reach the terrace. I again started climbing the final stretch of stairs, reached the terrace and closed the terrace door. The sun was slowly coming out in the sky. It was more than one day that my family had been trapped inside.

I was still clueless, not knowing how to get them all out. As soon as I reached the terrace, a blast happened from the top floor. The intensity of the sound was nail-biting. I fell down feeling the thunder it created. It almost shook the terrace surface and for a few minutes there was complete darkness in front of me. I took some time to regain my wits and later thought, *would Di be alright?*

I stood up slowly, holding my head and when I turned the other side, I saw a ladder rope. It was the property of the mall authorities, I guessed and used perhaps for lighting purposes during functions or for painting work. I took one end of the ladder rope and tied it as tightly as I could to one of the extended iron rods coming out of the terrace surface. After tying, I waited for the area down under me to be clear. And once it was clear, I could easily get down through the ladder. Meanwhile I thought of something which I hadn't thought about for the past one day:

So much has happened in the past 24 hours, but where is Iqbal?

Faces Unmasked

Tamanna got frightened and started screaming again when she saw the man entering. He looked very dangerous, his face covered with a dirty, brown mask. He was dressed in black trousers and a shirt with sleeves folded up. He started walking towards them. With each step he took forward, they took a step back. They both were in a state of fright, horror and aversion.

'You look scared, Aarav?' asked the man.

Aarav was in complete trauma after hearing his name from the man's mouth. 'How do you know my name?' he asked.

The man started laughing after hearing his question. 'C'mon Aarav, think a little deeper,' he said. Aarav still had no clue who he was, he still had no clue how he knew his name. He was completely confused.

'Who is he?' asked Tamanna with her trembling voice.

'Well, I don't think he will be able to answer it,' said the man. He lowered his gun and started opening his mask. 'Your memory is getting weak so quickly, I guess,' he continued while his face was now clearly visible. Aarav's mouth fell wide open. He was completely astonished, astounded, and perplexed. He was in a state of stupefaction after seeing his face.

'It's you!' said Aarav in a bewildered voice. 'Iqbal, it's you!'

'It's always been me,' replied Iqbal.

With a face of a peacemaker, Iqbal was a devil from inside. He was not an army man; rather, he belonged to the other side. He fooled us completely with his talks on patriotism and took us to commit an unforgivable sin. We believed him in all ways, we believed him in every aspect and by believing in him, we had betrayed everyone - our friends, our family, and most importantly...our nation.

'You cheat!' yelled out Aarav angrily and attacked him. He started punching him like a madman, releasing all his anger on him. Aarav was like a circus tiger who had been released from the cage.

'Aarav, stop!' cried Tamanna, who was standing and watching the entire scene.

Iqbal started blocking his punches and within no time, he kicked Aarav so hard that he collided with the row of flower cases. He hurt his backbone by colliding with one of the metal things kept there and was in pain.

'*Aaaaraaaaavvvv*'... screamed Tamanna, as she ran towards him to pick him up.

'How dare you stand against me?' said Iqbal, spitting a fleck of blood from his mouth and pointing the gun towards him. He was bleeding from his lips, a sign that Aarav had been really hard on him. For the first time, there was a soreness and rage in his eyes, something which he had kept under wraps for months in front of us. This was his real identity, a man prone to conniption.

'I'll kill you,' said Aarav still in anger.

'I wish you could, but now power is on my side.'

'You call this power?'

'You know what? You are pissing me off.'

'I don't fear cowards like you.'

'Really? Then this might give you fear,' said Iqbal, changing the direction of the gun towards Tamanna.

'Leave her, she has nothing to do with this,' said Aarav, holding Tamanna to his back.

'As I predicted, now you're scared of me,' said Iqbal as he smirked with a malicious smile. 'You know there's only one difference between love and power. Love makes a person weak who gives it a supreme importance.'

Tamanna was hiding behind Aarav, frightened out of her wits. She had no idea what was going on inside the shop, she only knew that their lives were on the verge of closure.

'You love her, right?' asked Iqbal, sensing Aarav's feelings.

'More than anything else,' replied Aarav.

Tamanna heard his answer and it was like all the fears she had till now had disappeared into thin air. Her tears stopped flowing and she felt as if she was breathing a new life, she felt as if she was standing at the edge of world from where she could take a big leap to her dreams. There was complete silence and peace around her. There was a blanket of calmness covering her.

'Then it might be painful to see her dying,' said Iqbal, walking towards them. The sound of his footsteps hinted that it was time for them to hear their death rattle.

'No, you can't do this,' said Aarav, struggling to get up. He was trying with all his might left within him to protect Tamanna.

'I can,' said Iqbal, 'it's really easy for me.'

'Kill me if you want, but let her go.'

'No!' shouted Tamanna.

'This is my fate; I need to face this,' said Aarav, looking at her. 'You should leave.'

'I cannot leave you, especially now when I know you too love me.'

'I'll continue loving you; I want you to be alive.'

'You both love each other so much; I am too excited about killing you both,' said Iqbal, sitting on a desk in a relaxed manner. He again wiped the blood flowing from his mouth and watched the two helpless humans that he could kill within a second, with no mercy and with no forbearance. Pointing his gun towards them both for the last time he asked - 'Answer me, do you both have hope that you will meet after death?'

'We live in each other's heart; you can kill us, not our hearts,' replied Aarav.

'Does she live in your heart?'

'Yes, she does.'

'Then make some space for these bullets too,' he said and pressed the trigger of his gun releasing a few bullets from it straight towards Aarav and Tamanna. The bullets hit their targets, making them tumble and collide onto the floor. They both lay facing each other and counting their last breaths. A stream of blood streaked out from their bodies and the light around them was beginning to fade. The darkness of their life was soon to arrive, a darkness that would never again show them the void of life. They both were still looking at each other, looking at each other alive for the last time.

'Have a good after-life,' said Iqbal, putting his mask back on, and getting out quietly.

Aarav slowly struggled to reach a little closer to Tamanna. After struggling for a moment, he placed his hand on Tamanna's hand and said with a struggling breath, 'I...uh...I-I love...you.'

'You...you are late,' said Tamanna, holding her fading life.

'Our love is pure and I didn't want to share it with you in this world. This is a dirty world, there's lot of commotion here, with lots of garbage all around. The garbage stinks and takes life. I didn't want this world to know about our love. They will find each and every way to separate us.'

'Then take me to your world.'

'It's not mine, it's ours,' said Aarav, reaching closer to her. He absorbed the excruciating pain caused by the deep wounds and continued, 'A world where there are no crowd of boundaries, no black clouds of sorrow. A world where there are only balloons flying in the air filled with your smile, where rain showers just to touch you, where prayers are said to heal your pain, where you sleep on the bed of peace and by seeing you, I ask to myself...am I in heaven?'

'Where is it?'

'It is there, where the blue sky ends.'

'I guess we are going there, promise me you'll meet me there.'

'I promise,' said Aarav, and with that he breathed for the last time, loosening his grip on Tamanna's hand. Seeing his life fading out, Tamanna slowly closed her eyes to meet him in their own world. They were among those lucky couples who died seeing each other's faces but they were also among those unlucky couples who tasted the pain of separation when they confessed their feelings.

The Black Cats were still in a state of war and were continuously fighting for our survival. I was on the terrace listening to all the firings, praying for it to end quickly.

Sir, this is Faiz, over.

Yes Faiz, what's the condition down there?

Bad, sir.

What happened?

We have two casualties here on the middle floor and both are kids.

God!

Sir, one of them... I know him, he was the one who came rushing towards us while we were entering the warehouse. He was yelling out to save his family.

How did he come in? Who's the other?

Don't know sir, it's a girl.

I thought middle floor was clear?

We had no idea they were here, sir, and enemy is still behind.

Take the bodies downstairs, over and out.

Over and out, sir.

Kabir Sir switched off his Bluetooth after talking with Faiz. He was still confused how there could be two dead people on the middle floor which they thought was clear. The commandos were slowly making headway; they had cleared half of the top floor, and rescued many hostages. They ordered everyone to remain inside till the area was completely clear and safe for them. Major Kabir, with his troops, was strong and harsh against the enemy camp.

'Sir, the theatre, screen number 4,' said Ram.

'Okay everybody, take your position,' said Major Kabir and he ordered his troop to break down the door. They blasted the door lock and entered.

'Give me cover,' said Major Kabir and he rolled in and straightaway started firing at the enemy standing in front of him. He was accompanied by his commandos and they didn't give a chance for the enemy to fire back at them. There were only three terrorists inside the movie hall; the rest were the hostages who were shouting in fear. The hostages included Di and my other family members. They were all rescued and quite safe now.

'Check the projector room.'

'Sir, we have a bag full of weapons here.'

'Take it and we should move on. I think this floor is done,' said Major Kabir.

'Yes sir,' replied Ram.

'You all just stay here until we return, don't come out,' said Major Kabir to all the hostages who were in the movie hall. 'The mall is still not safe for you to exit. We'll ensure no enemy crawls up here.'

It was almost 15 minutes since I'd heard the sound of a gunshot. I thought the area was clear enough for me to get down and slowly lowered the ladder. I started lowering myself slowly without looking down; I was really playing with the height factor. The crowd was roaring loudly at me, seeing my act. *Oh crap, they must be seeing me doing all this. I must be on the live coverage by now,* I thought. The front portion of the mall was completely made of glass. The blast that happened moments ago had damaged the glass pane of the top floor. When I got to the top floor, I was able to jump in as there was no more glass for cover. I got a bit injured while jumping in, as a piece of glass brushed my elbow and I began bleeding. I was playing with my life, one slip and I could have dashed onto the surface.

I could see the movie hall clearly in front of me in which Di and the others were kept. Without thinking much, I ran in. It was a huge relief seeing my family well and safe inside. I ran towards Di and hugged her tightly and cried out loud. Mihir, Youhaan, Avni, Suhaani and Sandhya also came and hugged me. We were all crying.

'Thank God you all are safe,' I said.

'How did you come here?'

'I'll explain it all later, first come with me.'

'Where is Aarav? Where is Tamanna?'

'Di relax, come with me,' I said and took them all towards the door. 'We need to get out of here as quickly as possible.'

'But the commandos advised us to stay here and moreover, there are so many people on all the floors.'

'We will get them all out,' I said but before I could say anything more, my mouth was closed by a hand that came from behind me. The hands got hold of me very tightly and tightened the grip on my mouth, leaving me struggling to breathe. The hands dragged me back and closed the door from the front. I could only make struggling sounds and hear Di and others screaming out my name loudly. Soon those hands left me and pushed me onto the floor. When I looked upwards to check whose hands they were, I found a mask on his face, a dirty brown mask.

Feeling Betrayed

Aastha Di, who's very fond of gardening, amazed us once with an outstanding fact that plants could do. It was evident that the biggest mistake of human beings was to consider plants as just immobile things on the planet.

'There are species of plants which are biologically shapeshifters,' said Di as she watered the plants gently using a watering can. 'I remember studying about them - the chameleon vines.'

'What are they?' I asked. 'What do they look like?'

'All I know that it's a climbing plant that has camouflaging abilities to mimic the leaves of its supporting trees. Without any contact, it can mimic a plant in terms of size, shape, colour, and spininess.'

I was totally awestruck after hearing that. I couldn't believe that the nature surrounding me had so much hidden within itself that no treasure of infinite gold could make up for it. Shapeshifters - I thought it was something restricted to only plants or animals until that man, holding the gun, removed his mask that day.

'Surprise...surprise,' he said with a dirty smile.

I was completely astonished, astounded, and perplexed. I was in a state of stupefaction after seeing the man's face. He was none other than Iqbal who had taught us the meaning of patriotism. I couldn't believe that I had been carried away by the talk of a person whose only hobby was destruction, whose only favourite visual was blood. Though not biologically, he turned into an army man and fooled us efficiently all these days.

'You're breathing heavily,' said Iqbal, coming nearer and crouching down.

'Why did you do this?' I said with all my voice I could muster.

'Nice question...is this the last wish before you die?'

'What?'

'God, you are sweating too much.'

He was talking to me with a soft voice but one that had a devilish intent in it. He was cutting my veins with his voice.

'I want your family members to scream louder than this and that will only happen when you die in front of them. Please don't think that I am not going to kill you. Believe me, it's as easy for me as I killed your brother, Aarav and his sweet love Tamanna, half an hour ago.'

His last line was another shock for me but this time the shock hindered me, it pierced, stiffened and solidified my blood flow. No nightmare could be more frightening than those last lines. Anger was slowly building up in me, it built up so much that I forgot he was holding a gun. I was about to attack and kill him, but he stopped me, placing his gun on my forehead.

'Don't you dare,' he said. 'Your brother did the same mistake and he paid for it. I am warning you, don't piss me off.'

'You coward!' I yelled out in anger.

'Don't shout, it's not good manners to shout at your elders.'

'Elder, my foot!'

'Well, in that case, I'll give you one more reason to shout at me. I killed your friend too; yes, I was the one who killed Prithvi.'

I was broken after hearing that. Paralysed, powerless, uprooted, wrecked and wounded. I started crying; my most beloved friend, who had nothing to do with this was now dead because of my fault. I was controlling my boiling anger, as he was still holding the gun on my forehead. The sight of my family members stopped me from doing anything outrageous.

'He had nothing to do with you,' I shouted.

'Yes, he had nothing to do with me until he interfered in my personal matter. As a matter of fact...' he folded his legs to sit comfortably and continued, 'I didn't like him at all. We closely followed the four of you and I didn't liked the fact that he was changing you guys.'

'What are you saying?'

'Well I give you the last five minutes of your life; ask me whatever you want during these five minutes.'

'Why did you kill him?'

'Then let me narrate to you, the last few hours of your friend's life.'

***

I rushed up, gathered all my family members and reached the terrace. I shouted, '*Prrithviiiiiiii...!*' He looked upwards and we all waved our hands goodbye. He waved back to us smilingly. Moving ahead, he walked a little distance ahead when suddenly, the mobile phone started ringing. He took the phone out of his pocket to check who it was, but the screen displayed an unknown number.

'Hello,' he said, swiping the white circle to the top of the screen.

'Hello Samarth...meet me near the puncture shop.'

Only two lines and the phone got disconnected. Prithvi didn't know whose voice it was. But he decided to go to that place instead of me. He decided to take the risk and check who it was. After reaching the spot near the puncture shop he waited for the caller to come. He was hiding in a tea stall for the time being. Fifteen minutes went past and nobody came. He was about to move when suddenly, the phone again started ringing.

'Where are you? I've been waiting here for so long,' said the voice on the other side.

'I am sorry, I won't be able to come.'

Prithvi kept him busy on the phone with some reason or the other while he searched for the caller. After walking a little distance, he noticed a man talking on his phone. He went nearer to the man to check if it was actually him to whom he was talking.

'I am not able to hear you clearly.'

'Hello...now can you hear me?'

He was the same man. He quietly disconnected the phone and kept it on silent mode. He stood nearer to the man and watched all his doings. The man was repeatedly dialling the number but couldn't get to it. Backing out finally he started walking and that's when Prithvi started following him. He followed him a long way till he diverted to a much narrower lane, so narrow that it was really difficult to walk properly among the crowd. The man took a turn into one of the buildings situated in the lane and started climbing up a few stairs. Prithvi followed him upstairs.

He saw the man opening the door of a room and getting in. He reached near the window and peeped inside but couldn't see anything other than dimmed yellow light prevailing inside the room. He tried to open the window slowly and as luck would have it, he was successful in opening it as it was not properly closed. He moved the curtain a little bit and saw a few men busy working on some electric circuitry, handling wires while some were checking arms and ammunitions. He wondered who they were. He took out the phone from his pocket and clicked the camera on. He made sure the camera sounds and flashlight was off and started clicking pictures of the happenings inside. While taking the photographs, he clicked a face that he had seen before. It was none other than Iqbal's face.

Prithvi recalled seeing Iqbal on the morning when we had a fight with him. He understood everything; he remembered the story that I told him about Iqbal and about how we were helping him. But he sensed something different. Seeing those men at their work, he suspected that Iqbal had not been truthful. Instinctively, he felt that he was doing something wrong. He switched to the video mode and began recording all the activity in the room. After collecting all the evidences that he could in that short time span, he closed the window and started moving out, but he was stopped by a voice.

'Who are you? What were you doing?'

Prithvi didn't answer his question and started running downstairs. The man behind him started shouting, 'Everybody come out,' and started chasing him along with his group. They ran continuously after him. Prithvi was struggling to run through the narrow lanes. He was running through a huge crowd. It was already 8:00 pm, and dark. The man and the group following him covered their faces under masks—dirty, brown masks.

Prithvi continued running but at one point, he collided with a man on the street. The collision decreased his speed and for his bad luck, he was caught by the man who was after him. They got hold of him tightly. He struggled to escape but the whole group had caught him. They dragged him to a place which was less crowded. Three of the men dragged him against the wall while one of them slapped him continuously. Prithvi was slapped so hard that he started bleeding. The man stopped slapping him and Prithvi saw a figure coming into the light slowly out of the darkness. He came nearer to him and stared at him with a harsh look that revealed his real identity—a merciless man.

'Today, you committed a great mistake,' said the man, holding Prithvi's hairs tightly.

'And you have committed mistakes your whole life,' said Prithvi, struggling fiercely to get out of the hold of his men.

'You are standing on the verge of your death, and still you're speaking with a lot of confidence.'

'I learnt never to fear people like you.'

'That's good,' he said and he took out a gun and continued speaking. 'This might help you to fear me.'

'At last, you've shown the sign of your cowardly nature.'

'How dare you talk to me like that?' and he pointed his gun towards Prithvi. 'Any last wish?'

'I want to see you dead.'

'Take him to the corner.' His men dragged him to an isolated corner. He still had the gun pointed towards Prithvi, his smile was still on.

'I hope your last wish will be fulfilled.'

He was about to fire at him when Prithvi suddenly thrashed his hand as a result of which he dropped his gun. That act disturbed his concentration and allowed Prithvi to run for his life again. The catch and chase resumed. Prithvi ran a long distance but it was no use—the brown masks were in no mood to leave him. The people watching them were shouting, but no one had the courage to stop what was happening.

Iqbal and his men ran a long way, but at one point they lost him. He was nowhere to be seen around. After searching for around fifteen minutes or so they stopped, seeing Prithvi in front of them. He was standing with his face turned the other side. They couldn't understand the reason why he had stopped suddenly. He was not even turning back and seeing the force of death standing behind him. It seemed as if he was looking at something in front of him, it seemed as if he was talking to someone. But all this was of no concern to the masked men; Iqbal again raised his gun, took perfect aim and shot a bullet towards him.

Prithvi lost his balance after being hit by the bullet. He staggered and leaned against a car parked in front of him. It seemed as if he was covering someone with his body. After waiting for a moment, Iqbal emptied his gun fully on Prithvi's back and he, with his struggling breath, pushed himself against the car and then again started running. But this time, he couldn't run as he was on the verge of death. His footsteps became slow and within no time, he crashed on to the ground, finally closing his eyes. A few people who were present there ran out and cleared the area quickly, saving their own lives.

'It's all clear, let's move out from here,' Iqbal ordered.

Prithvi was lying spiritless, anaemic and ashen. I didn't know my friend was taking his last breath somewhere in the middle of the capital as I peacefully slept in my home. I didn't know my friend would not be able to keep his promise of meeting us again the next day because he was dead—and it was my fault. He died to get all of us out of danger.

***

'With these hands, I killed him,' said Iqbal, as he narrated to me how he killed my friend.

Tears spurted out of my eyes when I heard him speaking about Prithvi's death. I was shattered to hear that, and I felt as if my own life was a burden for me.

'I don't know what all information would have gone out if he'd remained alive.'

I placed my hand on my pocket where my mobile was kept. He still didn't know that Prithvi had clicked so many photographs of them that night. He was completely clueless about it. Iqbal had only killed him, but he hadn't killed his hard work and brave soul. My job was to keep the photos safe with me; I didn't want to waste Prithvi's sacrifice.

'Why did he stop suddenly?' I asked.

'I don't know, maybe he was a fool or an over-confident person that he challenged death.'

I was not satisfied with his answer and with a heavy heart, I remembered that innocent face of my friend who met with death at such a young age.

The Finish Line

'**Y**ou all were never the part of the plan,' said Iqbal, answering my long list of questions before I die. There were only two minutes left before he puts a bullet into my head and ends my miserable life.

'What do you mean?' I asked.

'Let me elaborate...When I arrived in Delhi, my only motive was to threaten everyone, but I didn't know how to do it. I had a plan, but I didn't know how to execute it. Then you four met me by fate outside that internet café. You thought meeting me was a mere incident, but for me, it was the start of a long-awaited plan.'

'So, you selected us?'

'Yes, from that day onwards I was following you, each footstep of yours, I was spying on each and every moment of yours. A perfect opportunity knocked at my door when I found you four fighting with that over-confident friend of yours.'

'Don't spell his name from your foul mouth,' I shouted and was about to charge at him forgetting the fact that I was living on a few minutes of mercy.

'You're forgetting your manners, kid,' said Iqbal, shutting my mouth tightly and suffocating me. Seeing me struggle, he released his hands after a minute leaving me gasping behind. 'When I interacted with you all in that park,' he continued, 'my initial feeling was that you all were innocent kids but at the end of the conversation, I found that you were fools. You were so greedy for fame and recognition that within no time, you were in my trap. I didn't need to do any hard work to convince you.'

'Yes, we were fools that we agreed with you.'

'Uh...not yet,' he said, hinting that there was more evidence of our foolishness. 'A fool is not a fool until he commits the same mistake twice.'

I saw him laugh like a mad man after he said that. That laughter of his was so haunting that it would give me nightmares on every freaking night. 'When you told me your so-called safe place,' said Iqbal, 'I was surprised, because you made my plan easier. You kept all the bags filled with weapons in your school. We only needed to enter your school and take those weapons anyhow. Your school declared a day off for the sad demise of your friend. That day, we entered safely and the rest of the story, you know.'

'That's why you asked me where I hid those weapons?'

'You got me right.'

'I should have got you right before time.'

'Maybe you can fulfil that wish in another lifetime,' said Iqbal, getting up. It was about time that I close my eyes and meet the fateful death that awaits me eagerly.

'The bomb blast which took place that day was the work of my men; we were just having a net practice. The security in the city tightened a bit after that. When we came to know that you were chased by the police, we decided to have a break. Your friend Prithvi saved our plan by not telling the police that those four boys were you.'

'He saved our family from getting a bad name.'

'Well, that's another side of his over confidence,' said Iqbal. He held the collar of my shirt and forcefully pulled me upwards. 'He never really listened, isn't it? he asked, whispering in my ears. 'He only made you believe what he thought was right. And, that my friend was a sign of dominance.'

He pushed me to the front wall and continued speaking by aiming his gun. 'Your late friend was a growing dictator, my dear. I saved you from him and I shall save everyone in the same way. Capturing that bus, and straightaway heading here, to this mall was just the beginning of salvation.'

Where I battling with Iqbal, Inspector Kishen has been persistently trying to communicate with Major Kabir for the past few hours. He needed to provide him a very important piece of information. He was about to reach the limit of frustration when a policeman came running towards him saying - 'Sir, we've Major Kabir online.'

Sir, this is Kishen.

Kabir here, what's the outside report?

Sir, two boys have got inside the mall. You may remember them rushing to us while we were entering the warehouse.

They were two and I am afraid one is dead.

Oh God! Where's the other? I suspect he's on the top floor.

How do you know?

Minutes ago, we saw someone climbing down a ladder and breaking the glass of the top floor to enter inside. The crowd went berserk after seeing him.'

I need to find him, over and out.

'What did he say?' asked Aradhna Di after Inspector Kishen completed the conversation. She was closely following him and had overheard the conversation that happened.

'He'll try his best to find them,' he replied, not disclosing that terrible bad news.

'Faiz, you said that you found two kids dead, where are they?' asked Major Kabir, standing at the empty corridor of the ground floor.

'Sir, I found their bodies in that flower shop.'

Major Kabir and his men went to check the dead bodies on the second floor. The bodies were placed on the desks. Major Kabir went to check the first one and it was Tamanna. He went to the second one. It was Aarav and on seeing him, he said, 'Oh my God!'

'Sir, he was the one...' said Ram.

'I know,' he said, cutting his colleague short. 'I am afraid we might find the second body soon, too. We need to check the whole building again, come with me.'

Major Kabir split his men again into different groups and instructed them to reach the top floor from different directions. The end of a long running operation to counter the terrorists now rested upon a small doubt. Believing the words of a man who stood outside as a spectator was a risk, but he had no other choice.

Iqbal's mind was a victim of psychotic disturbance. I could clearly infer that from his words. He had so much rage and violence supressed inside him that he could've burned the whole world. He was walking around me like a tiger stalking its prey.

'It was never my intention to hurt you and your family, ' said Iqbal, loading his gun. 'But fate brought you all here. I call it a bad coincidence. Secrets have to be secrets. I myself am a secret. What guarantee do you have that you know my real name? Of course, it is fake, I lied.'

He wide opened his mouth and continued laughing. 'I have no name, no place and no identity,' he said. 'I'm just a face. In these last few seconds of the life you breathe I'll tell you one important thing - Nothing ever was real for you.'

He was not an Indian. Irrespective of the name, he belonged to a place where he was trained to die and not to live. Maintaining a distance of one hand, Iqbal pointed the gun at my chest and said, 'would you count these last seconds of your life or would it be my pleasure?'

I was not at all ready to die, especially by a man who was responsible for all the agony caused to my family. His gun end was on my chest and my heartbeats were faster than a bullet train.

'43, 42, 41, 40...' he started counting.

'You still think I am going to die?'

'What kind of question is that?'

I hit his nose with my full power, giving him a sudden jerk. He didn't expect such a hit from me because of which his nose started bleeding and the gun slipped from his hand.

'You swine, you shouldn't have done that,' he said, absorbing his pain. He picked up his gun and held me tightly not allowing me to run away. Flushed with rage, his jaws had tightened and his eyes blazed with fire. I was breathing heavily, my heart thudding wildly. He placed his finger on the trigger, smoothened his grip and then I heard a gunshot, a gunshot that ended everything.

For a minute, I thought that all my perturbations had come to an end, I thought I'd reached the exit door of the cycle of life and was about to enter into a new light. For a minute, I didn't hear a feeble sound around me, even the screams of my family members were mute for some time. Only the sound of the gunshot was echoing in my ears. I regained my senses to see what the reality was. I found a dead enemy, a man with no name lying dead in front of me. There was a deep hole right through his neck from which the blood had started to ooze out slowly. I took a minute to realize that he was dead, the betrayer was dead.

A complete silence had fallen. The atmosphere around me was soundless, reticent, hushed and zipped. I heard the sound of footsteps coming towards me. When I turned to the other side, I saw the commandos. I saw Major Kabir standing with his gun still pointed straight towards me. The hole through the enemy's neck was from his bullet. To be more precise, he had saved my life.

One hour later, every stranded and trapped person inside was successfully taken out into the air of freedom. All hostages were rescued, there wasn't a single enemy left who was alive and the biggest of them all was lying in the form of a corpse. The hostages were slowly moving out into the open air. I came out along with Di and others into the morning light that was not just a morning light, but the light of liberty and sovereignty. We had never imagined nor experienced such a situation. I started breathing normally when I stood with Di under normal and controlled circumstances.

This massacre had changed the face of the mall completely. Fumes coming out of all the floors, broken windowpanes, bullet holes on door surfaces, blood stains on the floor, crying faces, sunken souls and disheartening voices were the visuals in front of me. I felt as if the root of my life was mercilessly uprooted.

'Di,' someone suddenly called Aastha Di.

When we turned back, we saw Aradhna Di running towards her and giving her a tight hug.

'Thank God, you all are alright,' she said in a crying voice.

'Relax Aradhna, we are fine.'

Aradhna Di relaxed a little bit and started hugging everybody, one by one. She was very happy to see everyone fine and her tears were slowly drying.

'Samarth...why did you do that? Why did you enter inside? And...' she looked around me for a second and completed her question. Where's Aarav and Tamanna?'

I had an answer, but I didn't know how they were going to take it. I had no clue how they were going to digest the hard, dreadful truth.

'Speak up.'

'Di, they are...'

'They are what?'

'They both are no longer alive.'

I said it finally and as I knew, the truth was numbing, unbelievable. I was crying in front of them profusely. They all were standing emotionless and lifeless in front of me; they were standing like bodies made of earth but with no life or heart in them. I had no idea how to console them. The only thing left for me to do was to see them cry in despair.

On the other side, the dead bodies of some of the hostages were being taken out. That scene made me more daunted and crushed. But one particular scene had me beaten and crippled; I saw Aarav and Tamanna's dead bodies being taken outside on a cloth stretcher. At that moment I heard a huge crying sound around me. I realized that they also saw what I just saw.

I was totally broken after seeing them like this and I started running towards them, crying loudly and shouting, '*Aaarraaavvv...!*' But I was unable to reach them because the policemen stopped me. They held me tightly and didn't allow me to go further. I was struggling against them with all my force, desperately trying to loosen their grip, but I failed. Crying and yelling, I fell down to the ground, onto the dust of truth and onto the dust of greed. With tears still flowing from my eyes, I helplessly watched them in front of me, I watched them till they faded from my view, from my eyes and from this world. After a few minutes, the officers loosened their grip on me and allowed me to go.

I slowly stood up with my mourning face and wet eyes. My family, they were shattered into pieces and were crying and shedding uncountable tear drops. The whole atmosphere around me was burning in front of my eyes. I was clueless about my own presence.

A little distance ahead of me, I saw Major Kabir standing and regulating things. He was dealing with the injured hostages and arranging the dead bodies of the fallen enemy. I suddenly got reminded of something; I suddenly heard some words being echoed into my ears. Those words, I had heard them before too...*the answers to all our questions are just hidden around us, they are invisible until we are desperate to get them.* I had heard those words from Prithvi, he had told us the meaning of the words much before, but I understood it only at this particular moment. The question in my mind was, how to save my family's reputation? And the answer that I found was standing right in front of my eyes...Major Kabir.

Aftermath

I was found guilty on account of my confessions to Major Kabir and as my punishment, I was sent to juvenile reformatory for a definite period of time to be rehabilitated. My age can never be an excuse for the crime I committed. I deserved much severer punishment than spending some years in a juvenile home. It was my own realization that was speaking. After all, who'll forgive a person convicted of treason? One sinful man, like me, less in this world will make goodness weigh more on the scale of humanity.

Sitting inside this juvenile home, I still think of that day when I confessed everything and took on myself, all the responsibilities for the crime that had been committed.

'Sir, I want to tell you something,' I said to Major Kabir. 'I know how all this happened.'

He was stunned to hear that. 'What do you mean?' he asked.

'Sir, I mean I am also responsible for this massacre.'

He was again appalled and confounded after hearing what I said.

'Can you explain it to me in detail, for God's sake,' he said.

I narrated to him, the whole story - starting from the first meeting with Iqbal followed by the job proposal, how I did all the tasks assigned to me, how I was paid, how Prithvi died, how I came to know that we were cheated, and how I lost the important elements of my family. Taking all the blame on myself, I started crying after confessing everything to him. I didn't take the names of my brothers as I didn't want them to be punished. Their future deserved to be secured, for their betterment and for my paradise to exist.

It was me who thought that Iqbal would bring us fame, it was me who thought that what we were doing was right, it was me who convinced them to do all this, and it was me who was responsible for bringing disrepute to my school.

'I can't believe you did this,' said Major.

'I didn't know that I was digging my own grave, whatever I did, I didn't know that its outcome would be so harsh. It happened all because of my greed.'

'You were a fool,' said Major Kabir angrily. 'Don't you have the sense to know what is right and what is wrong? Even for a second, you didn't think that it was a trap?' He brought me to a corner, away from the people, and continued expressing his displeasure. 'We sacrifice our lives to protect this nation. When our own people do things like this it makes all our efforts go in vain.'

I deserved to hear more from him. I wish somebody had told me that sooner before this city had come to grief because of me. He shook me vigorously and said, 'don't you realize? You cheated yourself; you failed to identify the right path.'

'Failure is my habit, from the time I was born,' I said. 'I had only tasted failure. But I never failed intentionally; whatever happened was because of my unfortunate fate.'

'You have any idea how this will impact in your family?'

'I don't want my family to be involved in this; they have the right to live a peaceful life ahead. Please, sir.'

'As a protector and follower of the law, I need to do what is my duty. I have to take you in.'

'I know, sir. Here is my mobile,' I said, handing over that bad omen to him. 'It has all the clues and evidence about the massacre that happened here. With all respect to the bravery of my friend Prithvi who clicked this evidence, I hand it over to you. I have only one request; I need just a few minutes so that I can talk to my family.'

'Sure. Within some time, we will take you all to the hospital to attend to your injuries; I'll take you from there.'

'I'll follow whatever you say, sir.'

I went to the place where my family was standing, still crying after seeing Aarav and Tamanna's bodies. They never imagined that one day, they would see them in that state. I didn't know how to tell them that the hard times weren't over yet, here was a lot more to come. I took Mihir and Youhaan to one side and told them everything, whatever I had said to Major.

'We are ready to go with him,' said Youhaan.

'Not we, it's only me,' I said.

'What are you saying?' asked Mihir.

'I am the person who is guilty, not you, you all are innocent and have clean hands,' I replied.

'Listen, we did all this together, we can't let you do this alone,' said Youhaan.

'You have to let me go; it's my fate and I need to bow before it,' I said.

'That's not fair,' said Mihir, who started to cry.

'The thief has to win everyone's trust back,' I said, reminding Mihir about the lessons learnt from the story of Arab and the thief. 'For that he must surrender in front of the law.'

'But...still...'

'Look behind, there's a family that needs a shoulder to cry on; you'll be those shoulders upon which they can rest with ease. If you both come with me, they will be alone, deprived of any support, all they will get is humiliation.'

'You too are part of that family, we need you,' said Youhaan.

'It's better that there is one person less rather than all three. If you come with me, our brother Aarav will also be considered a criminal. No one will respect his death; there'll be no one to cry for him, there'll be no value to his lost life. At least for the sake of his soul, you need to obey me,' I said.

'Let me go instead of you,' said Mihir.

'No Mihir, Sandhya will not be able to absorb that shock,' I said.

'What about Avni then?'

'She'll be alright, one day she will realize that I was not wrong. But I cannot blame you all for my act of greed,' I said.

After much pleading, they allowed me to do what I had decided. They were destroyed and shattered due to my decision.

'Take care of everyone after I go. Tell Di everything that has happened with us, make her understand that what we did was just a mistake. And ask her if she could ever forgive me,' I said.

'Please don't go,' said Youhaan, crying.

'Don't worry. I am happy that my family is safe behind me, the only thing I regret is that it's not complete, I lost two valuable parts of it,' I said.

'Di will not be able to absorb this pain,' said Youhaan.

'She will learn to as time passes. Make sure that no one other than our family comes to know about this. No outsider should come to know what happened to us. I am not at all worried about my image, but I am worried about you all. People will not allow you to live peacefully there,' I said.

All the injured hostages were taken to the hospital immediately. The doctors treated everyone with utmost care. I had a minor injury on my forehead and elbow. After the treatment, I went with Major Kabir as per his orders. I made sure that no one in my family saw me while I walked out of the hospital. The commandos took me along with them, making sure that no one saw me. They were quite successful in protecting me from the media gathered outside. I went along with them to a place that I'd never seen before, that I'd never heard of before, that I never wanted to go to. Waiting for the coming dark life ahead, I only prayed for the well-being and safety of my family whom I'd left behind.

The court found me guilty and responsible for the crime committed. I was sent to live the next few years of my life in the Juvenile Reformatory. My identity was kept as a secret as per the laws of the Juvenile Act.

Continuing with my dark life there, I was provided with the facility of studying ahead. I belonged to the group of younger boys who always lived under the dictatorship of the senior boys. They made us do all their basic duties like washing their utensils and clothes. We struggled to get our share of food. The warden and the security staff never bothered to interfere. The rooms here were crowded. In the name of recreational facilities, only one small TV set was kept in the room. I used to gather information of what was happening in the outside world from the security staff who read newspapers daily. In return for his kind-heartedness, he assigned me to hide his liquor bottles.

I came to know that the government announced about Rs. 5,00,000 as compensation to each of those killed in the terror attacks and about Rs. 50,000 to the seriously injured. The bodies of many of the dead hostages showed signs of torture or disfigurement. I didn't know the exact number of attackers and hostages who were killed in that incident. People from all walks of life held candle-lit vigils at India Gate in the memory of those who lost their lives during these attacks. Not just in Delhi, people took to the streets to pay their respects all across the nation. Among them, the highest number were students. They even carried posters saying 'Protect Us', while some of them displayed 'We will fight back' or 'Abandon terror.'

My family also joined that movement—I came to know that as I saw Aradhna Di's photograph on the front page of a daily newspaper. In the photograph, I saw her standing in the middle of countless candles and holding a frame-like object. I knew at once that she must be carrying the photograph of either Aarav or Tamanna. I was happy that they all were fighting for justice to the deserving.

Again, talking about the life at the reformatory, the children living there had dedicated themselves to the life within. Even if they got out from there, it would be difficult for them to lead their old, normal life—but it would be easier for them to take their dark life to a higher level. Children are found in the homes even after the stipulated period, you may find one or the other stranded there for six years. You may also find someone who landed there for the fourth time.

I was restless and was desperate to get back home; I missed my home very much, so much that I could not even express it through words. The lovely face of my Di was circling around me; I often thought, if I could have backed out that fateful day, my life would have been different. Sitting in front of the only window of my room, spending sleepless nights, I thought of my mistakes, indecorum, and poor judgment.

I myself became the black shadow,

Of this sinister and infernal life.

The direction to which it goes,

I trace the same path behind.

I think of a lovely face,

The only remedy that I find.

A face that I see on the white lather of moon.

A face that takes me back to the road of hope.

A hope that I can still find my broken and missing wings.

Epilogue

The era of toddlerhood, innocence, learning, socialising, exploring, school, puberty, and adolescence was finally over and I stepped into the shoes of adulthood. The days of my life in juvenile home finally ended and I stepped out of the gate into the open air. I had stopped counting the days when it turned into years. There was no point in holding on to life when it had ultimately failed you. I didn't know what year it was or what the world had become. The winter that I knew had returned home already, and summer had freshly arrived in town with a different semblance. The nature before me, appeared new and fresh, as if I was seeing it after ages.

I saw Aastha Di in front of me. She was standing like a statue, silently watching me with tears in her eyes. I walked up to her slowly; she was, as usual, looking elegant with her ethereal beauty. She looked more beautiful, maybe because I was seeing her after a long time. She kissed my forehead, hugged me, and said, 'We missed you so much.'

'Same here, Di.'

We got inside the taxi, and it started to move. Watching the view outside, I felt as if I was back to my normal life. The streets of Delhi, those architectural marvels, the heritage monuments, and those festivals—I missed them all. I was reborn again in the same place, which I tried to destroy though unknowingly. I wish it could give me a corner to bury the remains of my wrong deeds and a chance to break new ground.

The taxi reached Jama Masjid. There was a little traffic ahead, due to which it moved slowly. I just turned my head towards the stairs of the Masjid, and I saw Aarav and Tamanna coming downstairs, holding each other's hands. They both were looking at each other with their eyes displaying serenity and endearment. The white light of peace and harmony covered them, making them the brightest of the stars. A gentle smile appeared on my face on seeing them. I couldn't make my mind understand whether they were real or just an illusion. It seemed as if God Himself was projecting his light of grace and playing his rhythm of concord. The driver honked. My reverie was disturbed, and they disappeared, making my eyes wander across the crowd. But I was happy thinking that they were still around me, in my own neighbourhood, like my own soul.

The taxi stopped in front of the three-storeyed building. My heart started brimming with emotions as I looked at my home. The building seemed as if it was newly painted, but I was sure that the people residing in it would still be the same. I missed my family. I was very eager and curious to see them, especially my brothers. Stepping out of the car, the first person I saw in front of me was Desai Uncle.

'Uncle, I've cleaned your scooter,' said Mihir as he came out of the parking shed. His legs froze; he stood like a man frozen in ice when he saw me. After seeing him, all the past memories started playing in my mind. All those moments of mischief, fun, joy, all came rushing back like a fresh morning breeze. My brother, who always made me laugh with his innocent behaviour, had tears in his eyes. He ran and gave me a tight hug. He was crying, with his tears falling on my shoulder.

'You learned to cry, Mihir?' I asked, pulling his leg and after a moment, he started laughing out. So did I. That time I was happy, happy to see my old Mihir back again.

'Di, Youhaan, Sandhya, everyone come out, look who is here,' shouted Mihir, looking at the balcony.

Sandhya appeared on the balcony hearing his shout. She looked at me and then ran inside shouting, '*Diiiiiiiii...*'

'You know what?' said Mihir, wiping his tears. 'Youhaan is training under a professional photographer as he has decided to convert his passion into a profession.'

'That's great, what about you?'

'I am continuing my studies; I want to pursue a career in law.'

I was enjoying the success of my brothers, I wanted to ask about everyone, but within a few minutes, my whole family was in front of me. Without wasting time, they all came and squeezed me with love. I was really controlling my brimming heart and obstructing my flow of tears. But that hug forced me to give up all, I started crying. Aradhna Di wiped my tears and said, 'No more crying.'

My family didn't reject me, they accepted me back. This was the biggest support I needed to get back into my life. And, continuing with the process of discovery, I learned my first lesson of adulthood. When you become an adult, you become philosophical rather than being a nag. I knew the road lying ahead before me would not be not easy to walk on; there would be hatred, ignorance, anger, anguish, and rejection waiting for me. But I was not in a mood to give up. Though the fight for my existence was going to be tough, though the struggle for getting back my place in this world was challenging, even then I'd keep on walking.

'You're forgetting something,' said Youhaan, bringing me back to the present.

'You didn't ask about Avni,' said Suhaani making me smile.

'She must be bathing, go upstairs and give her a surprise,' said Sandhya.

I started to walk upstairs by looking at my family behind, the best family anyone could ever have. Luckily, I could still break bread with them. When I add up more meaningful years to my age and grow a moustache, I could share a fortifying drink or dance to a delightful tune with them. When the rest of the world was coming close to materialistic things, I was becoming obsessive about my family.

Thinking about the girl whom I was going to meet within a few minutes, I remembered another night, many years back, when Avni gave me a surprise.

After having dinner, I was going to the terrace for a stroll. I was about to reach the terrace when suddenly a piece of black cloth covered my eyes.

'Who's that?' I asked stunningly.

Ssshhh... was the only thing I heard. 'Walk with me,' said the same voice, a girlish voice.

I followed what she said with two hands placed on my shoulder guiding me to the proper way. Stopping at a point, the same voice spoke to me again softly.

'When you walk beneath the stars and see the dwelling darkness so far...what do you hope for?' asked the voice, and the moment I heard it, I knew it was Avni.

'Light,' I replied and she took off the black cloth covering my eyes. I saw a row of candles a few steps ahead my foot, I wondered what it was.

'Light up the candles and bring some light,' said Avni.

We both went on our knees as she handed over the match box to me. I started lighting up the candles one by one and within no time, I saw three words in front of me. Those three words were not ordinary, they were special. I saw 'I love you' written with the help of handkerchiefs folded and placed accordingly. The candles surrounded them making a boundary. It brought a smile on my face.

'From where you brought these many handkerchiefs?' I asked laughingly. Honestly, I've always been a bit shy about expressing my feelings in this kind of situations and was trying to avert it.

'Wrong question, wrong time,' said Avni, which made me smile more.

'I love you,' she said, this time verbally. I opened my arms wide and she hugged me tightly. Her declaration made me feel special. Though I never said those three words back to her, she knew I spoke it inside, adding the word 'too'.

I came back to the present and stood at the doorstep of my house. The last time I saw this door was on that terrible day, the black day. I pressed the doorbell and was excited to see Avni once again. A minute later, the door opened and there she was, with the same simplicity. She was there to welcome me. Her hair was wet and so her eyes after seeing me. I walked closer to her, close enough to whisper in her ears.

'I love you.'

'Samarth,' she spelled my name and hugged me to never get separated again. The bitterness of my life was gone, and I engaged myself in filling that empty pool of honey again.

Two days later, we all left Delhi permanently. Aastha Di had already made all the arrangements to travel to a new city. I didn't ask anyone where we were going. All I knew was that I was leaving Delhi with lots of memories that I cannot fill in any bag. If destiny allows one day, I could trade in those memories for a nostalgia. And yes, destiny still remained a mystery until I requested Aastha Di to visit the Taj Mahal amid our journey. Just a temporary break to fulfil a long-forgotten desire.

We were at the Taj Mahal, the white marble mausoleum built by Mughal Emperor Shah Jahan in memory of his beloved queen, Mumtaz Mahal. I remembered reading in school that this jewel of Mughal art is a marvellous fusion of cultures, combining architectural elements from Persia, the Ottoman Empire and India. I had only heard from others that it is one of the most sacred symbols of love in the world, but I was witnessing it for the first time.

When I walked on one of the walkways of the Taj Mahal along with my family, it was still the same mystery of destiny that surprised me. A girl, admiring the monument of love, was walking beside me. My heart was heavy as I owed an apology to her. Though my simple apology could not compensate for her terrible loss, it would give me a sense of responsibility, to take care of her. It was Radhika. I requested her to accompany us in this trip to Agra. Her presence helped me to feel that Prithvi was still around me. I remembered him through her. Maybe the new place which was waiting for me would not offer me this blessing again.

Radhika looked quieter, more so now than when Prithvi died. I didn't know how she had felt when she came to know that she lost her love because of me. It may be because of Prithvi's good presence that she still didn't hate me. She must be definitely missing the winter season and her brown shawl.

We entered the interior chambers which were an octagon, with the design allowing for entry from each face, although only the door facing the garden to the south is used. As we moved in towards the graves, I saw Aarav and Tamanna again in front of me, surrounded with the same white light of peace and harmony. My mind again got confused as to whether they were real or just an illusion. But this time, they came to show me something, something which I never expected. Aarav pointed towards my right side and when I looked there, I saw Radhika standing alongside me. She was holding a piece of paper with her that she slowly handed to me. I took it with my trembling hands, unfolded it and read its contents:

He came to me like a story, each word of which was like my own voice. But before I could hear it fully, a page got detached from it and even today, I am searching for it.

Prithvi, he always astonished me, that day too, when under the starry night, he suddenly came and stood before me. As he had told me to meet him in the evening, I was waiting for him at the decided place. I told Meera about the place and the meeting, so that later, she could come and pick me up.

When he suddenly appeared in front of me, he was breathing faster. It seemed as if he was continuously running for a long time. There were signs of fear in his eyes, but one thing remained intact in its place—his smile. A smile that could bloom even the dry flowers, a smile which was made only for me. With a small distance between us, with the breeze so cold, with the night singing poetry, he slowly came near me and started to speak.

'Today you are looking very beautiful, so beautiful that I haven't seen you like this before.' He paused to catch his breath and then continued, *'Maybe because I might be seeing you for the last time and I may not be able to love you more. Whatever I say, just listen to it with the smile you have.'*

As soon as he said it, I heard a sound, a sound that stopped his words, a sound that made my heart again motionless, and a sound that ended everything. That sound caused a line of blood to flow from his chest, staining his shirt in red. He lost his balance and leaned on me against a car. His fast-moving breath was covering me. It seemed as if he wanted to speak many things to me but couldn't, because he knew something bad was happening to him. He took a long breath and again said:

'I wish that my life ends half an hour from now so that I can tell you these words with a rose in my hand. Radhika. Ana behibek...I love you. This life of mine is about to end, but I promise that I'll come back and lift you up in my arms.'

I was terrified to see him in that situation and was more terrified when I heard those horrible sounds again. Those sounds made his shirt redder, but his breath was still covering me. His eyes were almost about to close. He suddenly pushed me to one side and again stood straight. I almost lost my consciousness and in the fainting darkness around me, I saw him fading away into the distance.

When I opened my eyes the next morning in my home, I heard the hard truth that totally disturbed the balance of my heart and soul. I don't know what happened to me after that and I became the victim of darkness. My inner voice was lost because of that harsh incident. I lost my sense, not telling the world what I saw that night.

I refolded the letter and my hands trembled more after reading it. I came to know the reason why Prithvi stopped suddenly that day when death, in form of Iqbal, was behind him. Iqbal thought he was a fool, but the truth is, he stopped to complete his promise to Radhika. He stopped to tell her those words that she was most expecting. Tears came out from my eyes. The pain behind the tears I was shedding now was more than anything else I had been through.

'I wanted you to know the truth, that's why I wrote it for you,' said Radhika, taking the paper back. 'I don't have a reason for telling you this because I never told this to anyone.'

As she moved away, I saw a familiar face admiring the graves of the plain crypts. The face turned towards me and I said - 'Prithvi.'

He was like a guiding influence or a guardian spirit, acting as an intermediary between heaven and earth. He loved gifting happiness to others; he did that all the time, and was certainly doing it this time too. He was smiling at me, showing his thumbs up. He slowly walked towards me with his long hair flying in the air. He reached me and said softly:

'Aarav and Tamanna are safe, in peace in their own world. You look after your family; make sure they get what they deserve. And yes, take a little care of Radhika too. When you need any help, just look around for me.'

By the time I could figure out whether it was my pure imagination or not, he disappeared into the bright light. He was gone, with a promise to meet again. But I know that one day, somewhere ahead of time, he will rise again like a phoenix into a new life, facing a new sun. He was surely my most favourite subject in the course of life. I had learned a lot from him.

The end of my story should not be a sorrowful one; rather, it should lay the foundation for a happier tomorrow.

The way Prithvi lived his life, it taught me one thing—that when you put a bucket of hope into the well of dreams and pull it upwards with the rope of hard work, you achieve destiny. At last, standing on top of the heap of failures I cracked the code.

With the bright light suspending everything

Suspending darkness and spreading harmony,

I just want two wishes of mine to be fulfilled.

Before the globe takes another shift,

I hope to sleep without a nightmare.

And before I cry for my survival,

I hope to find an extended hand,

A hand for rescue.

A Note from the Author

The story of *Rescue* doesn't lay emphasis on what happened and how it happened; neither does it focus on who all are responsible. It lays emphasis on circumstances and how they affect the life of children. There may be many innocent kids who unknowingly got diverted to a wrong direction in their lives. There may be others who intentionally entered the dark world, choosing the last option available to them. Whatever may be the reason, they find it hard to regain their old, simple ways of living.

Samarth and his brothers don't represent any specific group of people, rather they represent a mindset. A mindset that can swing to both positive and negative sides. A heinous crime is a crime, whether committed knowingly or unknowingly. We need to create proper awareness in child education, we need to tell them what is right and what is wrong. We need to teach them how to identify people who will do good to them and who will change their mindset towards society.

There are many valid statistics and figures available which tell us to react immediately to this unfortunate situation of rising juvenile crimes. Let us pray that that every new child born in this land receive their much-deserved education, life lessons, and moral values. Let us hope that they emerge as visionaries, are guided by righteousness, and remain focussed on a better India.

About the Author

Shreejit Nair is a 1992-born Indian author, who has embarked on a writing career with *Rescue—Paradise to Inferno*, his first novel. Touched by the ecstatic poetry of Rumi and the extraordinary writings of Rabindranath Tagore, he started writing poems at an early age. His poems have entered Poetry Society's All India Poetry competition, Delhi Poetry Slam's Wingword Poetry, India Film Project's NaPoWriMo, and Notion Press Writer's contest. He was also a part of a screenplay writing contest for India Film Project (Season 8).